在我离开之前

[瑞典]
弗雷德里克·巴克曼
著

余小山 译

FREDRIK BACKMAN
OCH VARJE MORGON BLIR
VÄGEN HEM LÄNGRE OCH LÄNGRE

四川文艺出版社

所有的成年人都充满怒火，
只有孩子和老人才会哈哈大笑。

亲爱的读者：

我的一个偶像曾说："老去最可怕的地方在于，我的想象力也干涸殆尽了。"自从我第一次听到之后，这些字眼便在我脑海里萦绕不绝，因为这也是我最深的恐惧：在身体行将就木之前，想象力却已然枯竭。我猜有这样想法的人不止我一个。对于老去甚于对死亡的恐惧——人类可真是个奇怪的物种。

这是一个关于记忆和放手的故事，也是一个男人和他的孙子、一个父亲和他的孩子之间的书信和缓慢的告别。

老实说，我并不想让你读到它。我写下这个故事，只是因为我想试着整理自己的思绪，为了搞清楚自己的想法，我必须将它诉诸笔端。结果，它却变成了一个小小的故事，一个关于慢慢失去我所知道的最伟大的思想的故事，一个想念仍在这儿的人的故事，一个我想将其全部解释给孩子听的故事。因为它有这样的价值，所以我让它从我笔下倾泻出来。

这个故事书写了恐惧和爱，而大多数时候，这两者都相生相伴。最终，这个故事还是关乎时间的，哪怕我们仍旧享有它。谢谢你，因为你将这个故事赠送给了自己。

弗雷德里克·巴克曼

在我
离开之前

在生命的尽头,有一间病房。有人在病房中央搭建了一个绿色帐篷,一个人在里面醒了过来,呼吸急促,惊恐不安,不知自己身在何处。一个年轻的男人坐在他的身旁,轻声说:

"别怕。"

老人看着他的孙子,他想,这真是人一生里最好的时光呀!以诺亚的年纪足够看清世界运转的规则,但同时他也足够年轻,可以对这些规则不屑一顾。诺亚的双腿悬在长椅边晃来晃去,他的脚还够不着地面,可他的头脑却能抵达宇宙的任何地方；他来到这世上还不久，没人能把他的思想禁锢在地球上。他那垂垂老矣的爷爷坐在他身旁。爷爷太老了，老到人们已然放弃了他，懒得去数落他幼稚的举动；他太老了，老到别人再和他谈成长就嫌太晚了。到了这个年纪，说起来倒也不坏。

他爷儿俩坐在广场里的一条长椅上。诺亚迎着初升的太阳，用力地眨着眼睛。他不知道此刻他们身在哪里，但他也不想和爷爷确认。因为这是他们一直在玩的一个游戏：诺亚闭着眼睛，然后爷爷把他带到他们以前从未去过的地方。男孩会紧紧闭着双眼，有时爷爷带着他在市里换四趟公交车，有时爷爷带着他径直去他们家后面那片湖边的树林里，有时他们会坐进一条小船划很久，久得诺亚都睡着了。等小船漂到很远以后，爷爷轻轻地唤他睁开眼睛，递给他一张地图和一个指南针，叫他找到他们回家的路。爷爷知道，他总是会设法完成的，因为在这一生当中，爷爷对于两件事情的信念是坚定不移的：数学和孙子。在爷爷还年轻的时候，一群人计算着要如何把三个人运到月球上去，而数学帮助他们去了又回。数字总能引导人们归去。

可是这个地方没有坐标，没有路通到外面，也没有地

图可以指引到这里。

诺亚还记得今天爷爷让他闭上双眼，记得他爷儿俩蹑手蹑脚地走出房子。他知道爷爷带他来到了湖边，因为不管他是否闭着双眼，他都熟悉湖水的潆洄与歌唱。他记得他们踏进小船，能感受到脚底潮湿的木制船底，但在那之后，他就什么都不记得了。他不知道他和爷爷是怎么到了这里，然后坐在这个圆形广场的长椅上的。这个地方虽然陌生，但一切事物都是熟悉的，就像有人偷走了所有陪伴你长大的东西，接着将它们扔在一座陌生的房子里。不远处有一张桌子，就像爷爷办公室里的那张，上边放着一台小小的计算器和一沓方格信纸。爷爷轻柔地吹着口哨，音调悲伤，在一阵短暂的静默后，他柔声说：

"过了一晚，广场又变小了。"

接着，他又开始吹口哨。男孩看爷爷的神色有些困惑，爷爷这才第一次意识到他刚刚说那些话时太大声了。

"对不起，诺亚诺亚，我忘了想法在这里不是静默的。"

爷爷总是叫他"诺亚诺亚"，因为比起别人的名字，他对孙子的名字的喜欢是加倍的。他把一只手放在男孩的头发里，但并没有抚弄，而是静静地放在那里。

"没有什么可害怕的,诺亚诺亚。"

风信子在长椅底下怒放,无数片小小的紫色花瓣摇曳着,从花茎上长出的花枝挥舞着拥抱阳光。男孩认得那些花朵,它们都是奶奶的,闻起来有圣诞节的气息。对于其他孩子来说,圣诞节的气息也许是姜汁饼干味或者热红酒[1]味的,但要是你也有一个喜欢种些花花草草的奶奶,那么圣诞节的气息闻起来永远都是风信子味的。花丛中,有一些玻璃碎片和几把钥匙在闪闪发亮,就像有人把钥匙藏在一个大玻璃罐中,结果他摔了一跤,把玻璃罐落在了这儿。

"这些钥匙都是干吗的?"男孩问。

"什么钥匙?"爷爷问。

老人的目光忽而变得空洞起来,他沮丧地猛敲太阳穴。男孩张开嘴想说些什么,但看到爷爷这副模样后又戛然而止。男孩随即安静地坐好,看四周有没有什么地标或者线索。这是爷爷教他的,万一他走失了,他就得这么做。长椅周围是几棵大树,因为爷爷很喜欢树,因为树毫不在乎芸芸众生的想法。树丛中飞起一群鸟儿,它们穿过云霄,自由

---

[1] 姜汁饼干和热红酒是西方人过圣诞节时的主要食物与饮品。

地在风中飞翔。一条绿色的飞龙正神色困倦地穿过广场，广场角落里睡着一只企鹅，肚子上印着几个小小的巧克力色的手印，一只温和的独眼猫头鹰蹲在它的旁边。诺亚也认得它们，它们曾经都是他的。他刚出生时，爷爷就送给他一条飞龙。奶奶说，送给初生的婴儿一条飞龙当玩具太不合适了，爷爷却说，他才不想要一个仅仅"合适"的孙子呢。

人们在广场上四处走动，但每个人都模糊不清。当男孩试图把注意力集中在他们的轮廓上时，他们从他的视线里滑了出来，就像透过百叶窗的光一样。其中一个人停下来，朝着爷爷挥手致意，爷爷也摆出一副认识的样子朝他挥了挥手。

"他是谁呀？"男孩问。

"他是……我……我不记得了，诺亚诺亚，很久以前……我想……"

他陷入了沉默和迟疑，接着在口袋里搜寻着什么。

"你今天还没有给我地图和指南针呢，不用那些东西，我不知道怎么才能找到回家的路啊，爷爷。"诺亚轻声说。

"恐怕那些东西这次没法帮助我们了，诺亚诺亚。"

"爷爷，我们在哪儿？"

爷爷无声地哭了，却没有流下眼泪，连他孙子也没有察觉到他哭了。

"很难解释，诺亚诺亚，我真的无法向你解释。"

女孩站在他面前，她闻起来有风信子的气息，仿佛她哪儿也没有去过。清新的微风在她枯朽的发丝间吹拂着。他仍旧记得爱上她是怎样的感受，而那是即将离他而去的最后的记忆了。爱上她意味着在他的心里再也没有容纳其他人的地方了，所以他翩翩起舞起来。

"我们的时间所剩无几了。"他说。

她摇了摇头。

"我们还有来世，我们还有孩子和孙子。"

"我拥有了你，但只有那么转瞬的一刻。"他说。她笑了。

"你拥有我一辈子，我的全部。"

"那不够。"

她亲吻着他的手腕，下巴轻抚着他的手指。

"不是的。"

他们沿着一条路缓缓地走着，他觉得这条路他们曾经

走过，但不记得会通往何处。他安然地握着她的手，在那一刻，他们重返十六岁，他们的手指不再颤抖，心脏不再绞痛。他的胸口告诉他，他能跑到地平线去，但呼吸了一口气后，他的肺却不再服从自己。她停了下来，耐心地扶着他的手臂等待着。现在，她老了，就像她离开他的那一天。他在她眼前轻轻地低语：

"我不知道该怎么跟诺亚解释。"

"我知道。"她说。她的气息萦绕在他的脖颈间。

"他现在很大了，我希望你能看看他。"

"我会的，我会的。"

"我想你，我的爱人。"

"我仍和你在一起，亲爱的你，深陷难处的你。"

"但只在我的记忆里了，只在这里。"

"没关系，这里一直都是我最喜欢你的地方。"

"我去过这个广场的所有地方，过了一晚，它又变小了。"

"我知道，我知道。"

她用一块柔软的手绢擦拭着他的额头，血迹沾染在手绢上，仿佛红色的圆形小花在绽放。她责备他：

"你在流血。你每次进船的时候,都要小心一点儿。"

他闭上眼睛。

"我该和诺亚说什么?我该怎么向他解释,在我死之前我就会离开他了?"

她托起他的下巴,和他亲吻起来。

"我亲爱的丈夫,深陷难处的丈夫,你只要像解释其他所有事物一样和我们的孙子解释这些就行了,他可比你聪慧多了。"

他紧紧抱住她。他知道一场雨就要来了。

爷爷说出"很难解释"的那一刻,诺亚看到他脸上露出了羞愧的神色,因为他从来没有对诺亚说过这句话,但其他的大人会,就像诺亚的爸爸,每天都有很多事物"很难解释",但爷爷从来不会。

"我不是说,对你而言这些很难理解,诺亚诺亚,我是说,对我而言这些很难理解。"老人抱歉地说。

"你在流血!"男孩哭了。

爷爷的手指在额头上胡乱地擦拭。就在爷爷的眉头,一滴血悬挂在伤口上摇摇晃晃,像是在和重力进行拉锯战。

最终，它还是落了下来，滴在了爷爷的衬衫上。随后又是两滴血飞快地落下来，就像孩子们从码头上跳海一样，总要有第一个勇敢的孩子先跳，其他的孩子才敢接着跳。

"是的……是的，我应该在流血，我肯定是……摔倒了。"爷爷沉思着，像是突然想起了什么。

但没有什么想法在这里是静默的。男孩睁大了眼睛。

"等一下，你……你在船里摔倒了，我现在想起来了！你就是这么受伤的。我去叫了爸爸！"

"爸爸？"爷爷重复道。

"是的，爷爷，不要担心，爸爸很快就来接我们了。"诺亚拍着爷爷的手臂安抚着他，信誓旦旦地说道。就他这个年纪而言，他的生活阅历远远超过他这个年龄的孩子应有的水平。

爷爷的眼眸中透露着焦虑，男孩只好坚决地继续说：

"你还记得有一次我们去一座岛上钓鱼，睡在帐篷里时你说过的话吗？'有一点儿害怕并不是什么错事，'你说，'因为要是你尿裤子了，尿臊气能让熊熊都躲开。'"

爷爷用力地眨着眼睛，像是目光中诺亚的轮廓已经模糊了一般，随后老人点了点头，眼神又恢复了澄澈。

"是的！是的！我说过，诺亚诺亚，我说过这些话，是不是？那时我们在钓鱼，哦，亲爱的诺亚诺亚，你已经长这么大了，这么大了。学校的生活怎么样？"

诺亚的心在惊慌地跳动，他努力忍住声音里的颤抖，好让自己的话显得无比坚定。

"很好，我的数学成绩在班上是最好的。爷爷，放松下来，爸爸很快就来接我们了。"

爷爷把手放在男孩肩上。

"很好，诺亚诺亚，很好。数学总会指引你回家的。"

男孩害怕了，但他知道还是不要让爷爷看出来的好，所以他叫道："三点一四一！"

"五九二。"爷爷迅速地回答。

"六五三。"男孩接着脱口而出。

"五八九。"爷爷笑了。

这是爷爷另一个最爱的游戏——背诵圆周率小数点后的数字，这是计算圆周长的关键数学常数。爷爷沉醉于它的魔力，这些关键的数字解锁了秘密，将宇宙万象展现给我们。他能记住圆周率小数点后的两百位数字，而男孩只能记住他的一半。爷爷总说，男孩的思想在不断地膨胀，而爷爷的却在萎缩，终有一天，岁月会让他们记住的数字一样多。

"七。"男孩说。

"九。"爷爷轻轻说。

男孩紧紧握着他粗糙的手，爷爷看出了他的害怕，于是爷爷说：

"诺亚诺亚，我有没有跟你说过那次我去看医生的故事？我说：'医生，医生，我在两个地方弄伤了我的胳膊！'医生回答：'所以我建议你不要去那些地方嘛！'"

男孩眨眨眼，事情变得越来越模糊不清了。

"你之前说过，爷爷，这是你最喜欢的笑话。"

"哦。"爷爷有些羞愧，低声应了一声。

广场是一个完美的圆形，风在树梢呼啸而过，斑驳的落叶在飞舞着。爷爷最爱的就是每年的这个时候。暖风在风信子的花枝间吹拂着，爷爷额头的血滴已经凝固了。诺亚轻抚着他的额头，问："我们在哪儿，爷爷？为什么我的毛绒玩偶动物都在这个广场上呀？你在船上摔倒的时候发生了什么？"

爷爷的眼泪终于从他的睫毛上滑落："我们在我的大脑

里，诺亚诺亚，每过一晚，它就变得越来越小。"

泰德和他的爸爸在花园里，花园里弥漫着风信子的芬芳。

"学校的生活怎么样？"爸爸粗声问。

他总是问这个问题，可泰德总是不能给出正确的答案。爸爸喜欢数字，但男孩喜欢英文字母，这完全是两种语言。

"我的作文得了最高分。"男孩说。

"数学呢？你数学得了多少分？要是你在丛林里迷路了，那些单词能指引你回家吗？"爸爸咕哝道。

男孩没有回答，他不懂数字，或者说数字也许也不懂他。他爸爸和他，父子俩从未用眼神交流过。

他的爸爸——这个年轻的男人弯下腰开始拔花床间的杂草。当他站起身来时，天已经黑了，但他发誓赌咒明明才过了一小会儿。

"三点一四一。"他含含糊糊地说，声音变得不像他自己的。

"爸爸？"这是儿子的声音，但变得更低沉了。

"三点一四一！这是你最爱的游戏！"爸爸吼道。

"不是的。"儿子喏喏地回答。

"这是你的……"爸爸刚要说,却又把话咽了下去。

"你在流血,爸爸。"男孩说。

爸爸朝着他眨了眨眼睛,随后又摇了摇头,夸张地窃笑起来。

"啊,这只是擦伤罢了。我有没有跟你说过那次我去看医生的故事?我说:'医生,医生,我弄伤了我的胳膊……'"

他陷入了沉默。

"你在流血,爸爸。"男孩耐心地回答。

"我说:'我弄伤了我的胳膊。'哦,不对,不对,等一下,我说……我记不起来了……这是我最喜欢的笑话,泰德,这是我最喜欢的笑话。别再拽我了,我还能讲我最喜欢的血腥笑话!"

男孩小心翼翼地握住他的手,但这双手越来越小了。

而男孩的手却像两把铲子。

"这是谁的手?"老人喘着气问。

"这是我的手。"泰德说。

爸爸摇着头,血从他的额头上流了下来。他的眼睛里盛满了愤怒。

"我的儿子在哪儿?我的小儿子在哪儿?回答我!"

"坐一会儿吧,爸爸。"泰德恳求道。

日薄西山,爸爸的目光追寻着树顶的落日。他想哭,却不知道该如何哭,只能从喉咙里发出嗞嗞声。

"学校的生活怎么样,泰德?你的数学成绩怎么样?"

数学总能指引你回家……

"你得坐下来,爸爸,你在流血。"男孩恳求他。

男孩已经长出胡楂了,爸爸摩挲着他的脸颊时,能感受到他根根挺立的胡楂。

"发生什么事了?"爸爸低声问。

"你在船里摔了一跤,我告诉过你不要再去船里了,爸爸,那里太危险了,尤其是当你带着诺——"

爸爸忽然睁大了眼睛,激动地打断了他的话:"泰德,是你吗?你变了!学校生活怎么样?"

泰德缓缓地呼吸,一字一句地说:"我不再去学校了,爸爸,我已经长大了。"

"你的作文得了多少分?"

"坐下来,求你了,爸爸,坐下来。"

"你看起来很害怕,泰德,你为什么这么害怕?"

"别担心,爸爸,我只是……我……你不能再去船里了,我跟你说过千百次了……"

他们不在花园里了,现在,他们在一间没有味道的有着白色墙壁的房间里,爸爸的手轻抚着他满是胡楂的面颊。

"别怕,泰德。你还记得我教你钓鱼的时候吗?我们在一座小岛上,住在帐篷里,你必须睡在我的睡袋里,因为你晚上做了噩梦,还尿了裤子。你还记得我跟你说过的话吗?尿裤子是好事,因为尿臊气能让熊熊都躲开,有一点儿害怕并不是什么错事。"

爸爸在一张柔软的床上坐了下来。那张床很新,像是有人制造了它,但从未在上面睡过觉。那不是他的房间,泰德坐在他身旁,老人把鼻子埋在儿子的头发里。

"你还记得吗,泰德?那座岛上的帐篷。"

"在帐篷里和你一起的不是我,爸爸,是诺亚。"儿子轻轻说。

爸爸抬起头,注视着他:"谁是诺亚?"

泰德温柔地抚摸着他的脸颊。

"爸爸,诺亚是我的儿子,你是和诺亚在帐篷里。我不喜欢钓鱼。"

"你喜欢！我教过你的！我教过你……我没教过你吗？"

"你从来就没有时间教我，爸爸，你无时无刻不在工作，但你教过诺亚，你教过他所有事情。他也很喜欢数学，就像你一样。"

爸爸的手指在床上来回地摸索着，他在口袋里找着什么东西，动作越来越狂乱。当他看到儿子的眼中噙满泪水时，他的目光又转到了房间的角落。他紧握着拳头，指关节都握得发白了，好让他的手不要乱颤。他恼火地沉吟："但是，学校的生活怎么样，泰德？告诉我，在学校都发生了什么？！"

在爷爷的脑海中，一个男孩和他的爷爷坐在一张长椅上。

"在这个脑海里很美妙，爷爷。"诺亚鼓励地说。因为奶奶之前总说，要是爷爷忽然安静下来，你就说一些称赞的话，这样他就会继续说下去了。

"你真好。"爷爷微笑着，用手背擦干了他的泪花。

"就是有一点儿乱。"男孩咧着嘴笑了。

"你奶奶去世时，这里下了很久很久的雨，从那以后，我就再也没有让这儿恢复如常了。"

诺亚察觉到长椅下的地面上满是泥淖，但钥匙和玻璃碎片还在那儿。广场不远处是一片湖，湖面上涟漪阵阵，小船行驶过的痕迹消失得无影无踪。诺亚还能看到远处小岛上的绿色帐篷。他想起黎明他们醒来时，缥缈的雾气曾笼罩了整片树林，就像每个黎明他们醒来时盖着的薄凉的被单。每当诺亚害怕睡觉的时候，爷爷总会拿出一根线，线的一头系在他的胳膊上，另一头则系在男孩的胳膊上。他跟诺亚保证，要是诺亚做噩梦了，就拉一拉绳子，爷爷会立刻起来带着诺亚去一个安全的地方，比如码头上的一艘船上。每个夜晚，爷爷都遵守诺言。诺亚的腿悬在长椅旁晃来晃去，飞龙在广场中央的喷泉旁沉沉睡去。遥远的地平线上，一小群高楼大厦坐落在海岸上，周围是一片像是刚刚坍塌的废墟。那几座剩余的高楼笼罩在一片闪烁的霓虹里，外面零零散散地被几根绳子捆绑着，像是饥肠辘辘或急着上厕所的人随意把它们系着。浓雾中，忽明忽暗的灯光勾勒出图形，诺亚意识到，高楼上面写着字。一座高楼上面写着:"重要!"另一座高楼上写着:"记住!"但在最靠近海滩的那座最高的楼上,灯光闪烁的字是"诺亚的记忆片段"。

"那片高楼是干什么的呀,爷爷?"

"那里是档案馆,是留存所有事物的地方,所有重要的事物。"

"比如呢?"

"我们做过的所有事,拍过的照片、看过的电影,还有你那些无用的礼物。"

爷爷笑了,诺亚也笑了,他们总是赠送彼此一些无用的礼物:爷爷送给诺亚一个充满空气的塑料包当圣诞礼物,诺亚就回赠爷爷一双凉拖鞋。到了爷爷的生日,诺亚送给爷爷一块自己咬过的巧克力,那是爷爷的最爱。

"好大的一座楼。"

"那是一大块巧克力。"

"你为什么要紧紧握住我的手,爷爷?"

"对不起,诺亚诺亚,对不起。"

广场喷泉的周围是一片坚硬的混凝土石板地,之前有人用白色的粉笔在上面草草地写满了数学算式,但面容模

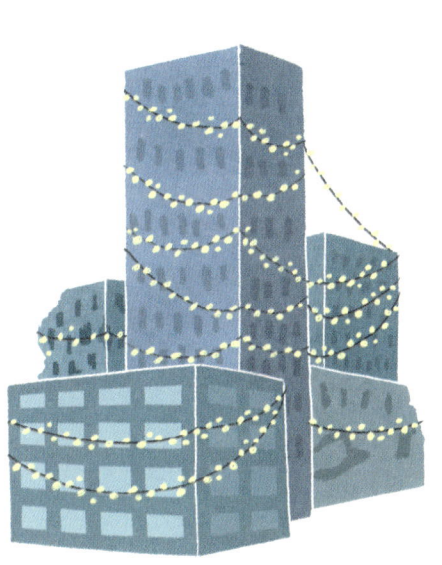

糊的人们在上面走来走去，他们的鞋底将数字一个一个地擦掉了，最终只残留了一些胡乱的横线，深深地印刻在石头上，变成了石化的等式。飞龙在睡梦中打了个喷嚏，结果它的鼻孔里喷出成千上万的纸片，上面写着什么东西。纸片在广场上纷纷乱舞，一群从童话书里出来的小精灵在喷泉旁飞舞着，竞相追逐着纸片。诺亚的奶奶曾给他读过那本童话书。

"那些纸片上都写着什么？"男孩问。

"写着我的念头。"爷爷回答，"它们都被吹散了。"

"它们已经被吹散很久很久了。"

男孩点了点头，伸出手紧紧握住爷爷的手指。

"你的大脑是不是生病了？"

"谁告诉你的？"

"爸爸。"

爷爷的鼻子呼出一口气。他点点头。

"我们什么都不知道，真的，我们对于大脑如何运转知之甚少。它现在就像一颗将要熄灭的星星——你还记得我教过你的吗？"

"当一颗星星将要熄灭的时候，要等它最后一束光经

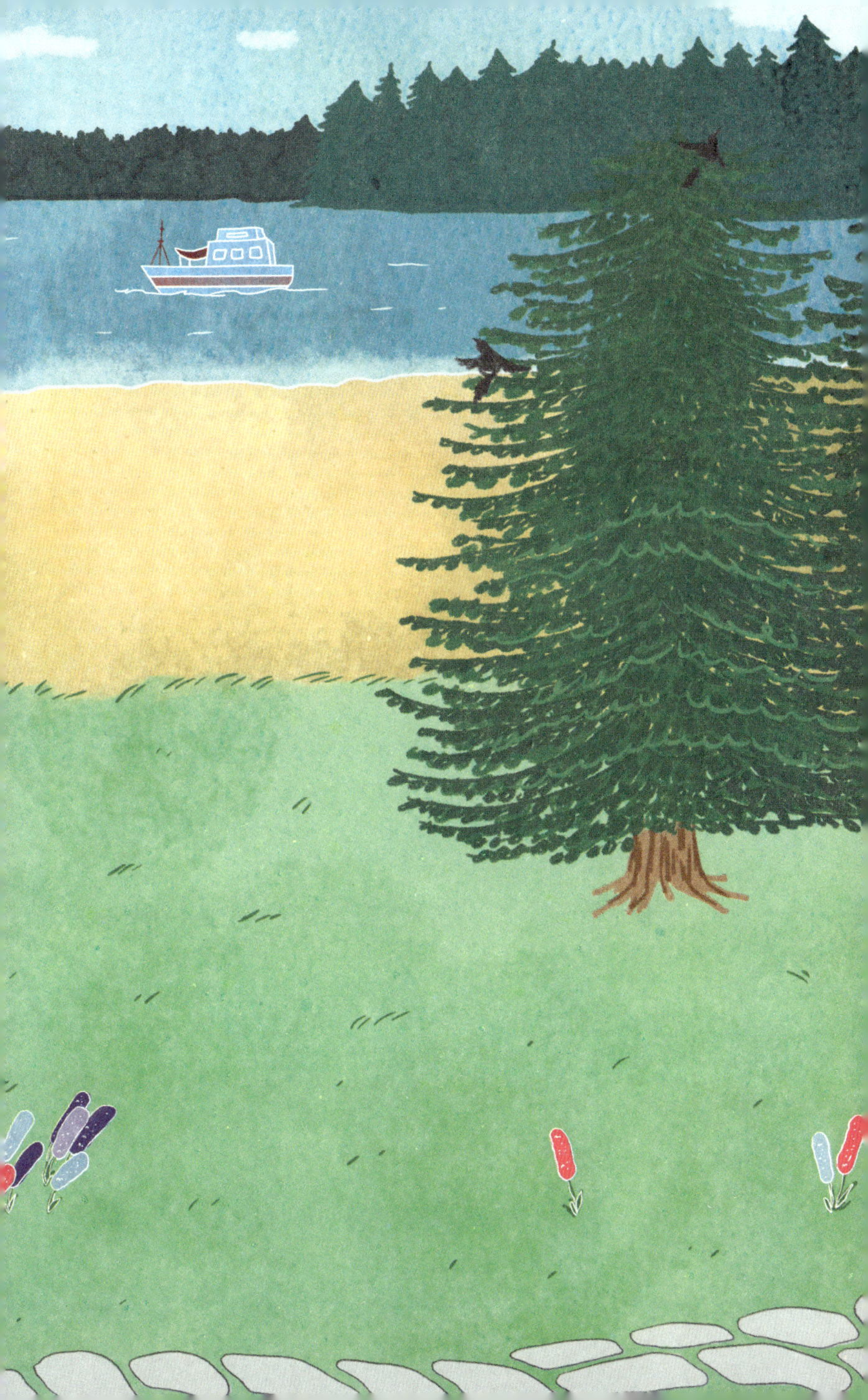

过漫长的时间抵达地球后，我们才会知道。"

爷爷的下巴颤抖起来。他经常告诉诺亚，宇宙有超过一百三十亿年的历史。奶奶曾经总说："你总是慌慌张张地看着这些东西，却连洗碗的时间都没有！"

"那些活得匆匆忙忙的人会错过很多东西。"她偶尔也会对诺亚这么说，不过那时诺亚还不懂，他要等到奶奶去世以后才会懂。爷爷紧紧握住他的手，好让他别再颤抖。

"当大脑开始凋零时，身体要花很长时间才会意识到。人类的身体遵循着一套庞大的运行体系，它是数学大师，直到最后一刻，它都在永不止歇地工作。我们的大脑蕴含着无穷的方程式，每当人类解出一道，它就会比我们去月球的那会儿更加强大。宇宙间没有比人类更神秘的了。你还记得我跟你说过的关于失败的故事吗？"

"只有当你再也不想尝试了，你才算失败。"

"很对，诺亚诺亚，很对。伟大的想法永远不会被禁锢在地球上。"

诺亚闭上眼睛，把眼泪憋在眼睛里，用力让它们倒流回去。广场上开始下起雪来，这场雪下得像是小孩子在哭泣一样，刚开始无声无息，随后就变得永无止境似的。厚

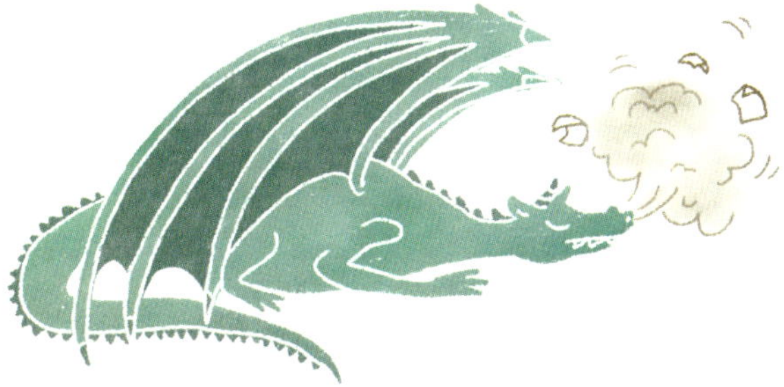

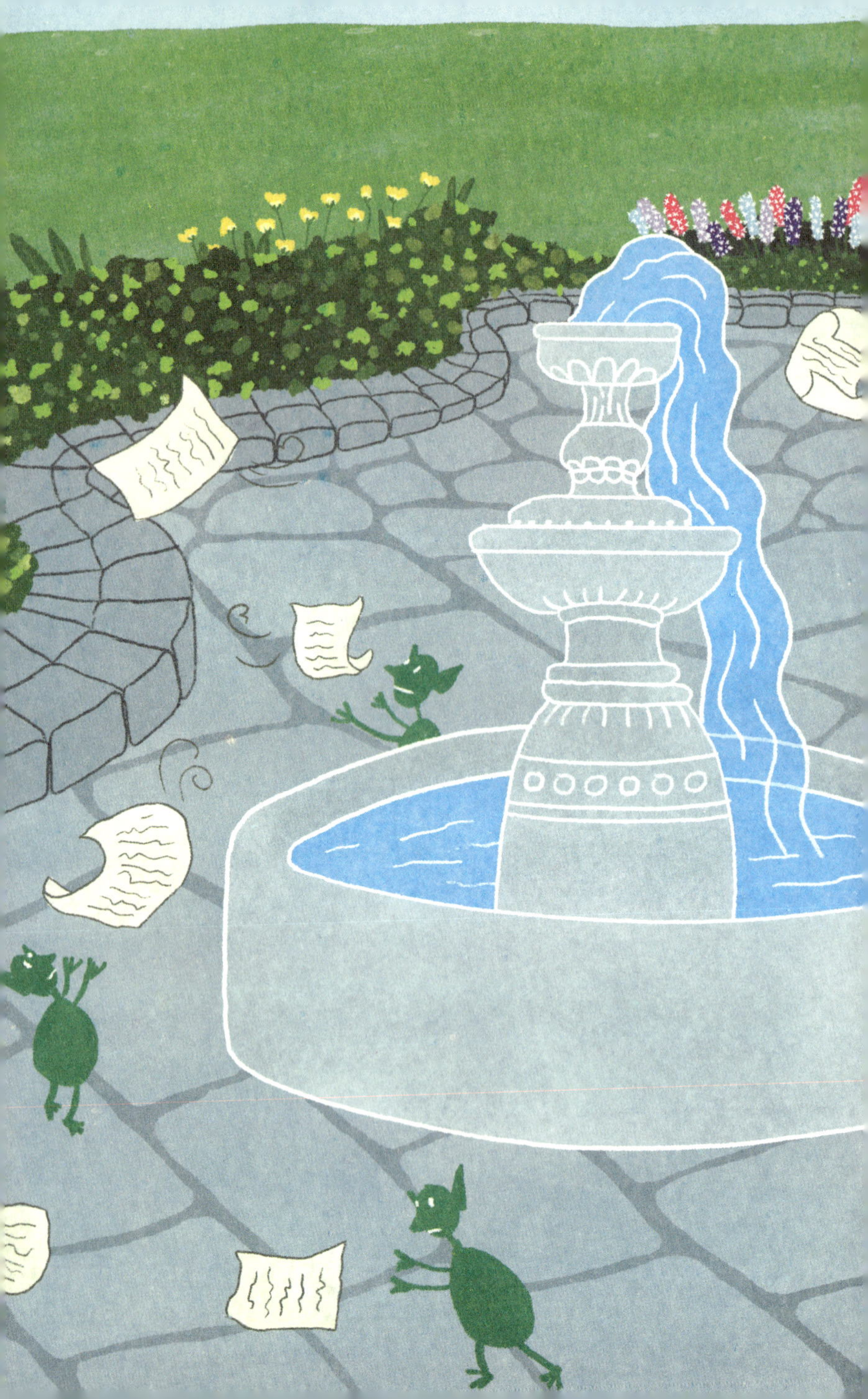

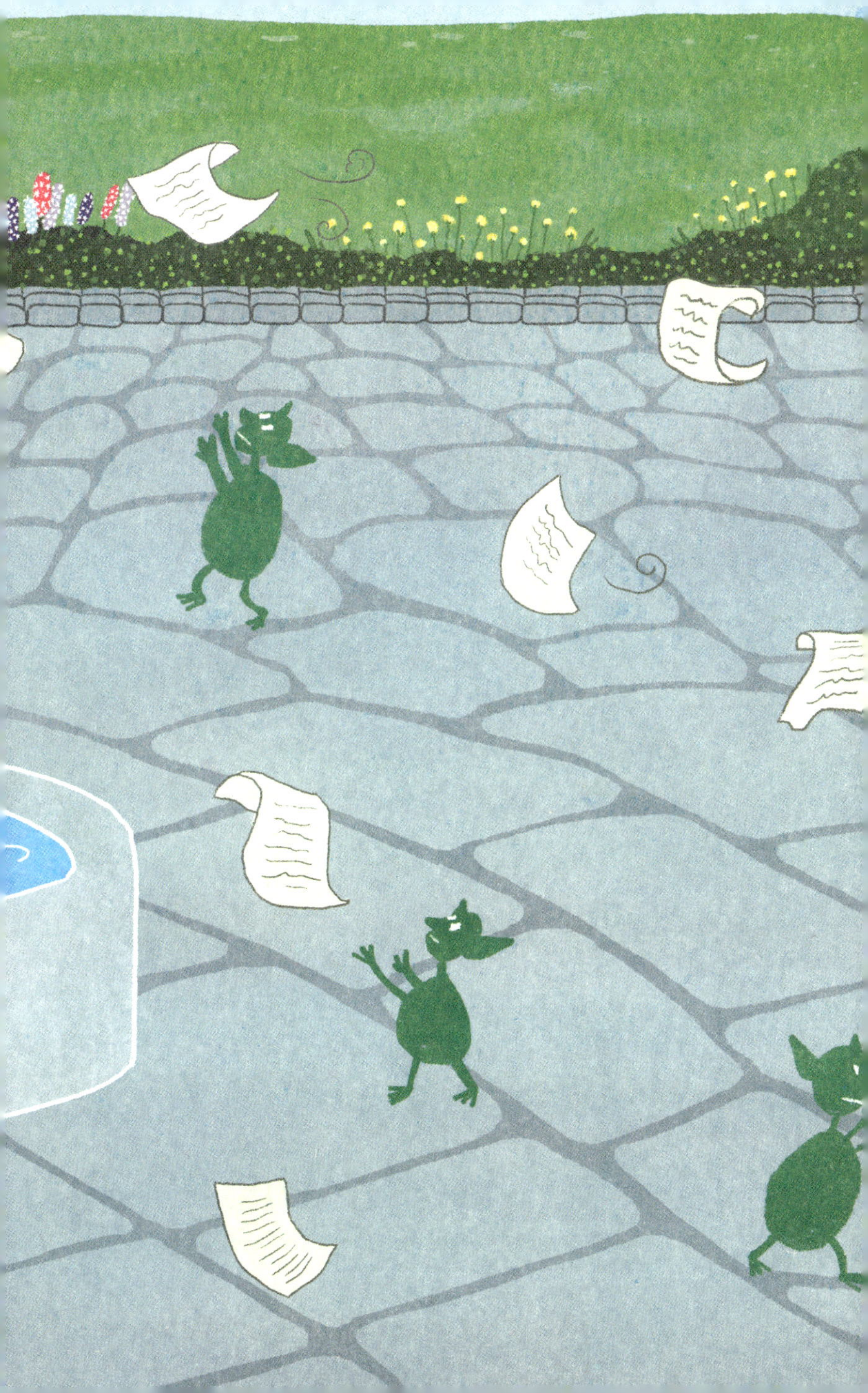

重的白色雪花覆盖了爷爷的思想。

"跟我讲讲学校的事吧,诺亚诺亚。"老人说。

他总是很想知道关于学校的所有事情,但不像其他大人一样,他们只想知道诺亚的表现如何。爷爷想知道的却是整所学校里发生的事,他从来没有听过的。

"我们老师让我们写一个故事,讲一讲等我们长大了之后想成为什么样的人。"诺亚告诉他。

"你写了什么?"

"我写,我想我还是先专心致志地做个小孩子吧。"

"这是个好答案。"

"是吧?我宁可变老,也不想变成一个成年人。所有的成年人都充满怒火,只有孩子和老人才会哈哈大笑。"

"你是这么写的?"

"是的。"

"你们老师说什么了?"

"她说我还没懂作业是要我们写什么。"

"然后你说了什么呢?"

"我说她不懂我的答案。"

"我爱你。"爷爷闭上眼睛说。

"你又流血了。"诺亚说着,伸手抚摩爷爷的额头。

爷爷拿出一条褪色的手巾擦拭额头。他在口袋里摸索着什么,随后又盯着男孩的鞋。男孩的双脚悬在柏油路上方晃来晃去,投下两片不规则的阴影。

"什么时候等你的脚碰到了地面,我就会在天外的太空里,我亲爱的诺亚诺亚。"

男孩饶有兴致地和爷爷打着节拍呼吸,这是他们的另一个游戏。

"我们是要在这儿学习如何告别吗,爷爷?"最后他问。

老人挠了挠他的下巴,沉思良久。

"是的,诺亚诺亚,我怕是这样的。"

"我想,告别总是艰难的。"男孩很坦诚。

爷爷点着头,轻轻摩挲着他的脸颊,可他的指尖却像干燥的绒面革一样粗糙。

"你是从奶奶那儿学到的吧。"

诺亚想起来了,那些夜晚,爸爸到爷爷奶奶这里来接他回去,他们都不准他跟奶奶说那些字眼。"别说那些话,诺亚,你敢跟我说那些话!你要是离开了我,我就老去了。

我脸上的每道皱纹都在向你诉说着离别。"她以前这样抱怨过,于是他转而给她唱了首歌,把她给逗笑了。她教他读书,教他烘焙藏红花小面包[1],教他怎么倒咖啡不会洒出来。每逢她的手忍不住哆嗦时,男孩就自己倒剩下的一半咖啡,这样奶奶就不会把咖啡洒出来了。以前倒咖啡要是洒出来的话,奶奶会羞愧的,而他再也不想让奶奶在他面前感到羞愧了。"我对你的爱,诺亚,"每当她给他读完那本讲精灵的童话书,他准备睡觉的时候,奶奶就把嘴凑到他的耳边告诉他,"连天空也容纳不下。"她并不完美,但她是属于他的。她去世的前一夜,他还为她歌唱。跟爷爷恰好相反,奶奶的身体将要罢工时,她的意识仍然清醒。

"我不擅长告别。"男孩说。

爷爷咧嘴笑了,露出所有牙齿。

"我们还有很多机会去实践,所以你会擅长的。周围走来走去的成年人对于告别都有一种遗憾,他们都希望可以回到过去再一次好好告别。我们的告别不需要这样,你会不断地与人告别,直到你会完美地告别。一旦你的告别

---

[1] 瑞典的传统圣诞食物,是一种发酵的甜面包卷,用金色藏红花和深色葡萄干调味。

变得完美，就是你的双脚能触碰到地面的时候了，而那时我会到太空里，到时就再也没有什么可害怕的了。"

诺亚握着老人的手，这个老人曾教他钓鱼，叫他别害怕那些奇思妙想，让他仰望夜空，让他明白夜空是由数字组成的。从这种意义上来讲，数学保佑了这个男孩，因为他再也不会畏惧其他所有人都会害怕的"无穷"这个概念。

诺亚热爱着宇宙，因为它永无止境，永生不死。在诺亚的一生中，它是唯一不会离开他的。

他摇晃着双腿，研究着花丛中那些闪闪发光的金属。

"钥匙上面刻着数字，爷爷。"

爷爷往长椅边探过身去，静静地看着它们。

"是的，确实是，上面有数字。"

"为什么呢？"

"我不记得了。"

他的话里忽然充满了恐惧，他的身体变得很沉，声音变得虚弱，他的皮肤像一张在顺风之中肆意的船帆。

"为什么你握我的手握得这么紧啊，爷爷？"男孩再次轻声问道。

"因为一切都在消失啊，诺亚诺亚，我一直握着你的手，就是希望你可以存留的时间最长。"

男孩点点头,他更用力地回握住爷爷的手。

他握着女孩的手越来越紧,越来越紧,她只好温柔地一根一根松开手指,亲吻他的脖子。

"你这么握着我,就像我是根绳子一样。"

"我不想再失去你了,我再也受不了了。"

她无忧无虑地在他身旁沿着这条路走着。

"我就在这里,我一直在这里。再跟我讲一讲诺亚,告诉我他的全部。"

他的表情一点一点地放松下来,然后他咧开嘴笑了,说:"他现在很高,很快他的脚就能碰到地了。"

"那你得要在锚下多垫几块石头了。"她边笑边说。

他喘不过气了,只好停了下来,靠在一棵树上。树皮上刻有他们的名字,但他不记得为什么要刻了。

"我的记忆正离我而去,我的爱人,就像你试着把油和水分离一样。我一直在读一本书,但总是缺了一页,那一页对我来说却无比重要。"

"我知道,我知道你很害怕。"她说,然后用嘴唇摩挲着他的脸颊。

"这条路会通到哪儿？"

"家。"她回答。

"我们在哪儿？"

"我们回到了我们相遇的地方。那边是一座舞厅，我们在里面跳过舞，你还踩过我的脚趾。还有那边是一家咖啡馆，我不小心把你的手指夹在了门里，导致你的小拇指至今还弯曲着。你还说过，我想跟你结婚可能只是因为我对此还抱有歉意。"

"我不在乎你为什么要和我结婚，我只在乎你现在是不是还在这儿。"

"那儿是一座教堂，我们就是在那儿结婚的。那里是一座房子，后来成了我们的家。"

他闭上眼睛，任凭他的鼻子去为他指引道路。

"你的风信子，它们从来没有像这样芬芳过。"

五十多年以来，他们拥有彼此。直到最后一天，她仍旧像是第一天在树下看到他那般厌恶他身上的某些特性，但同时也爱慕着他其他的品质。

"当我七十岁的时候，你注视着我，我跟十六岁时候

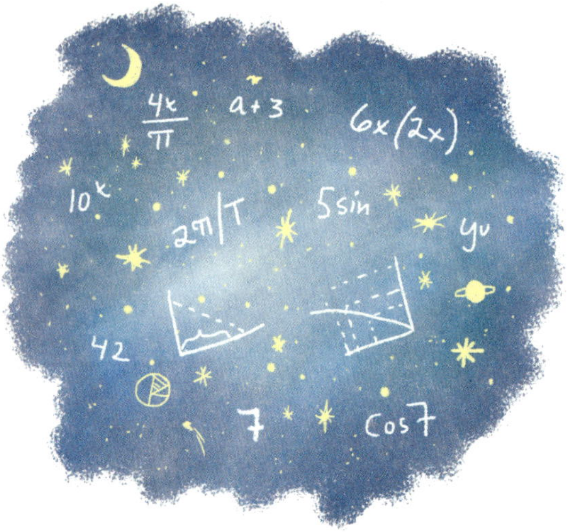
a+3
6x(2x)
2π/T
5sin
42
7
cos7

的感觉一样，深深爱着你。"她微笑着说。

他的指尖抚摩着她的锁骨。

"你对我而言，永远都是非凡的，我的爱人。你就是一道闪电、一团烈火。"

她轻轻地咬着他的耳垂，弄得他痒痒的。她说："没有人可以要求更多。"

没人像她一样跟他吵过架。他们第一次争吵是关于宇宙的，他跟她解释宇宙是如何诞生的，可她不信。他提高嗓门儿，于是她恼火了。他不明白为什么，她朝他大叫："我很生气！因为你认为这个世上的一切都是偶然的！但这个星球上有无数的人，而我偏偏偶然与你相遇。所以要是你说我也能偶然地与别人相逢，那我真的难以接受你那残忍的破数学！"她紧紧地握着拳头。他站在那里呆呆地看了她几分钟，然后他告诉她他爱她。那是第一次，从此以后他们就没停止过争吵，但也从来没有分开睡过。他穷尽所有的工作时间去计算概率问题，而她却是他最不可能遇见的那个人。她让他彻底改头换面。

他们搬进了他们的第一座大房子。在那黑暗的几个月里，他埋头在花园种植，当阳光照射进来，这座漂亮的花园终于敲开了她的心扉。他这么做是有信念的，他认为只有科学才会调动一个成年人，因为他想展示数学可以是美丽的。他计算着阳光照射的角度，绘图示意出树林遮挡的阴影，每天坚持记录气温，选择最好的植物种植。

"我想让你知道。"爷爷说。

"知道什么？"奶奶赤脚站在六月的草地上哭着问。

"知道方程是有魔法的，公式也是有魅力的。"

如今他们老了，就站在这条路上。

她靠在他的衬衫上对他说：

"然后，每一年你都会偷偷种一些香菜，就是为了惹我生气。"

他晃了晃胳膊，摆出了一个无辜的手势。

"我不知道你在说什么。我忘了很多事情，你知道的，我是个老男人。你刚才是不是说你不喜欢香菜？"

"你一直都知道我很讨厌香菜！"

"那肯定是诺亚种的，你可千万不要相信那个男孩。"他大笑。

她踮起脚尖，两手抓住他的衬衫，两眼定定地看着他。

"你并不简单，亲爱的你，生闷气的你。可你也不圆滑，你甚至很容易让人觉得反感，可没有人，绝对没有人敢告诉我你不会去爱。"

　　这座有着风信子及偶尔有香菜芬芳的花园的另一头，是一片很老的农场。农场里面，就在树篱笆的另一头，有一艘破破烂烂的渔船，是邻居很多年前拖到岸上来的。爷爷总说，他在房子里工作的时候得不到安宁和平静。奶奶也说，爷爷在房子里工作的时候她也得不到安宁和平静。于是有一天早上，奶奶出去了，到了花园的树篱笆旁，把那艘渔船装饰成了一间办公室。从那以后，爷爷在里面工作了很多年，四周环绕着数字、方程和等式。地球上只有这么一个地方可以让他有逻辑地思考万事万物，数学家需要这么一个地方，也许其他所有人也需要。

　　渔船的一边倚着一只巨大的锚。泰德还很小的时候，有一天他突发奇想问他爸爸，还有多久他才会比那只锚要高。爸爸冥思苦想着他什么时候才会比锚高，连他脑海中的广场都开始震动起来。他已经得到了教训，诺亚出生时，身为爷爷的他和身为爸爸的他已经是完全不同的人了。对于数学家来说，这并不稀奇。所以当诺亚问了泰德曾经问过的问题时，爷爷回答："你还是期盼着长得没有锚高吧，

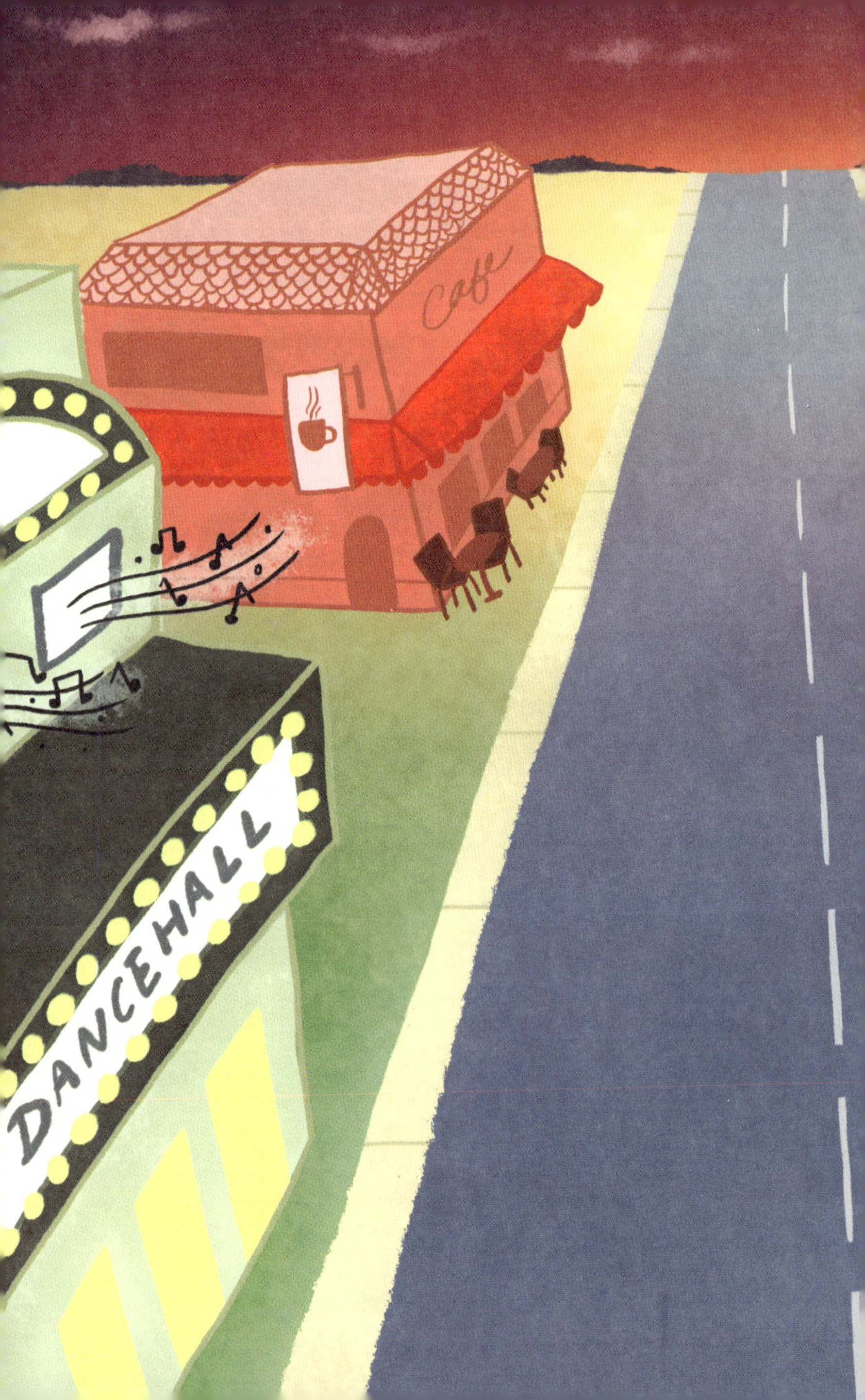
Cafe
DANCEHALL

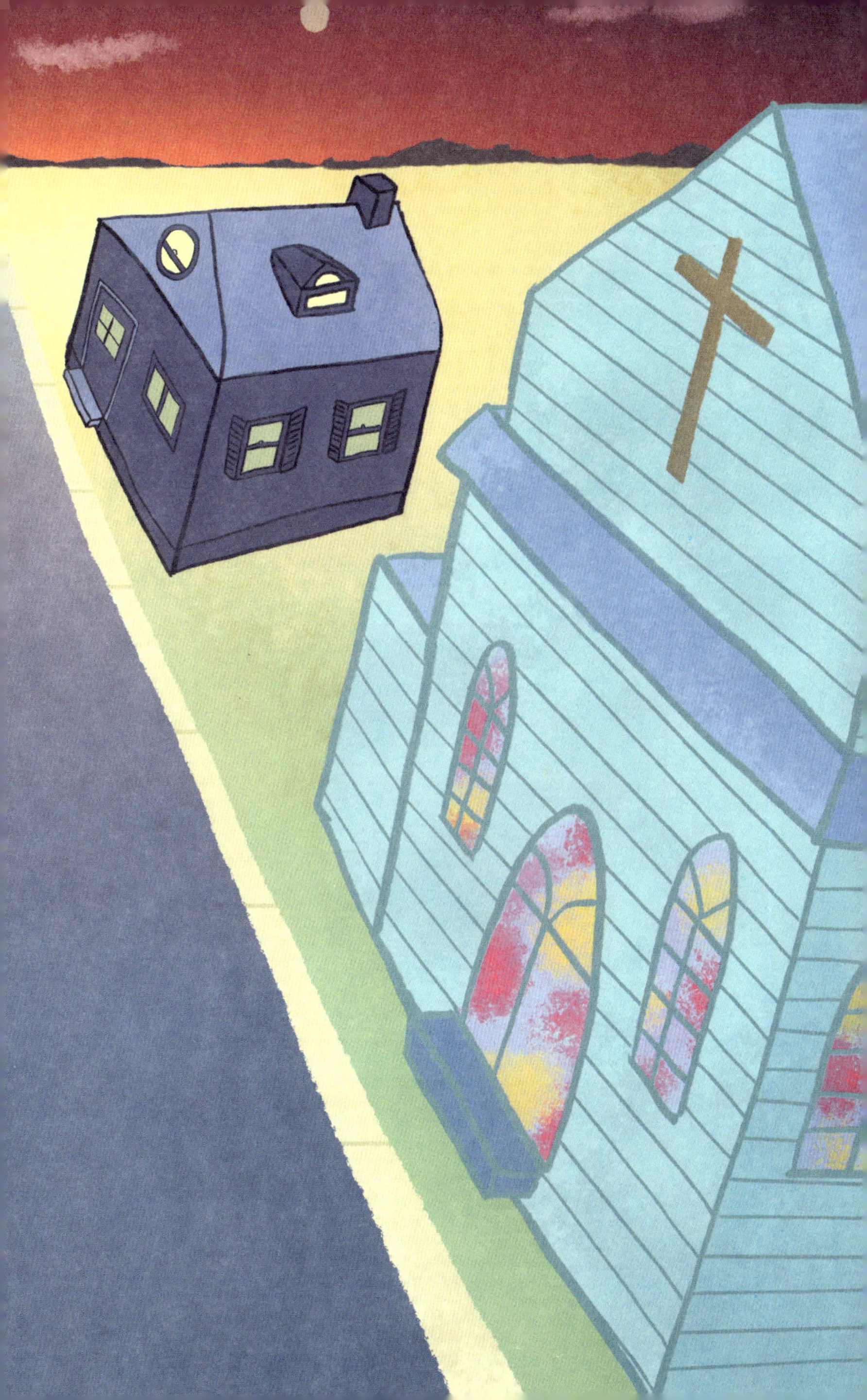

因为只有比锚矮的人才能随时去我的办公室里玩。"当诺亚的个头儿和锚差不多高时，他就在锚的底下垫块石头，这样他就永远有理由可以让诺亚来办公室里烦他了。

"诺亚越来越聪慧了，我的爱人。"

"他一直很聪慧，你还要花点时间才能赶上他呢。"她哼了一声。

他的话到了嘴边："我的大脑开始萎缩了，每过一晚，广场就变得越来越小。"

她揉着他的太阳穴。

"你还记得吗，我们刚开始相爱的时候，你说睡觉就是一种折磨。"

"是的，因为我们不能分享彼此的睡眠。每个早晨，当我睁开双眼，有那么一瞬间我竟不知道我在哪儿，我难以忍受，直到我知道你就在我身旁。"

她亲吻着他。

"我知道，每个清晨回家的路都越来越长。但我爱你是因为你的大脑，你的世界曾经要比别人的都大得多，辽阔得多，即便记忆离你而去，它们也剩余很多。"

"我太想念你了。"

她微笑着，眼泪滴落在他的脸庞上。

"亲爱的顽固的你啊，我知道，你从不相信有来世。但你应该知道，我是多么、多么、多么希望你错了啊！"

她身后的路越来越模糊了，地平线上正下着一场雨。他用尽全力抱着她，深深地叹了一口气。

"若我们在天堂相遇，你还要怎么与我争论啊？！"

一个靶子靠在墙上，旁边是三块写着植物名字的牌子，上面沾着潮湿的泥土。

地上躺着一个袋子，袋子里装着一副眼镜，一半的镜框露了出来。一台显微镜被忘在脚凳上，一件白色的外套挂在挂钩上，底下露出一双红色的鞋。爷爷就是在这儿，在喷泉旁向奶奶求婚的，奶奶的东西仍散落在各个地方。

男孩小心翼翼地抚摸着爷爷额头上的肿块。

"还疼吗？"他问。

"不，不怎么疼。"爷爷回答。

"我是说在心里，心里还疼吗？"

"越来越不疼了，这就是遗忘带来的好处之一，你忘记了那些让你痛苦的事情。"

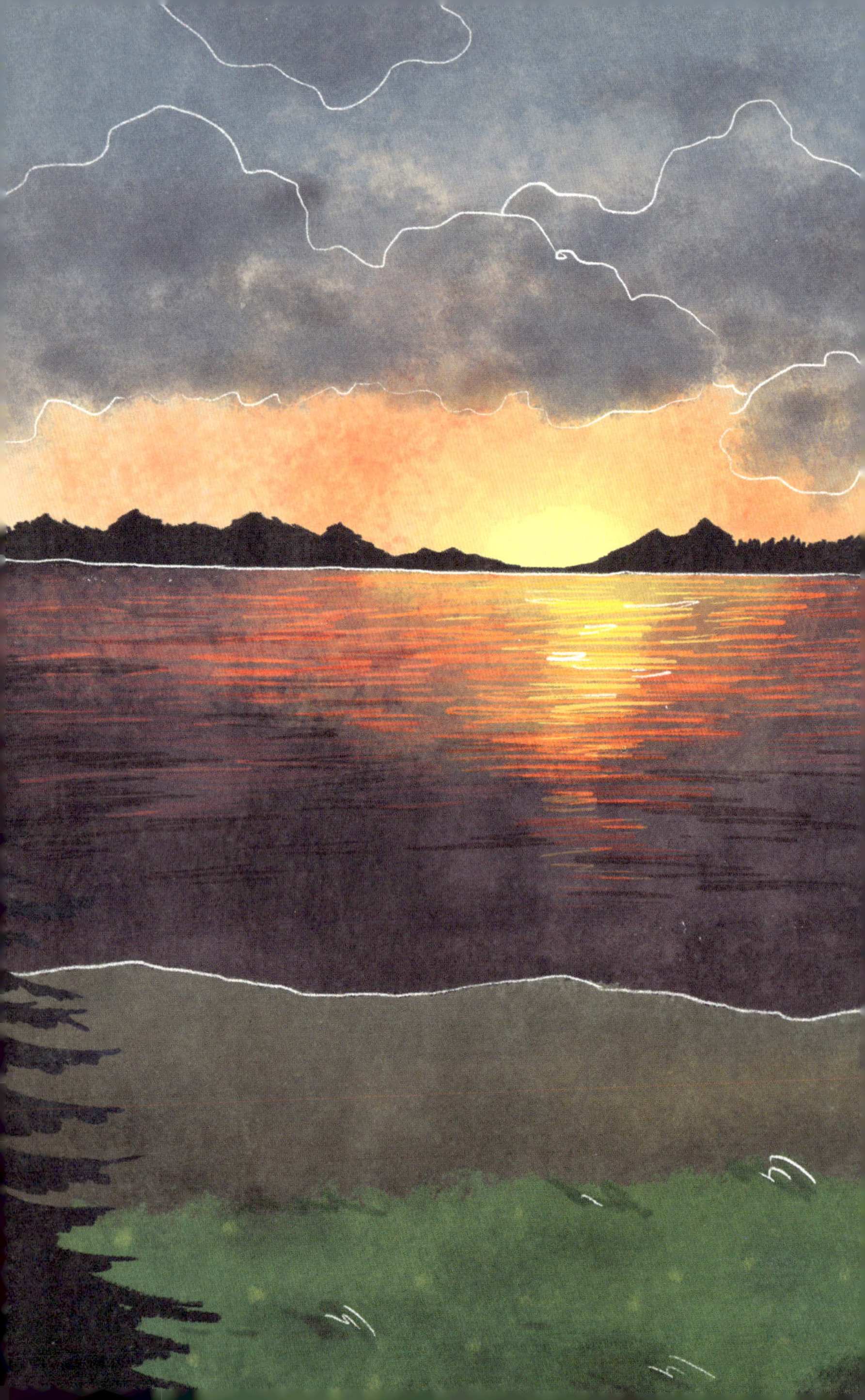

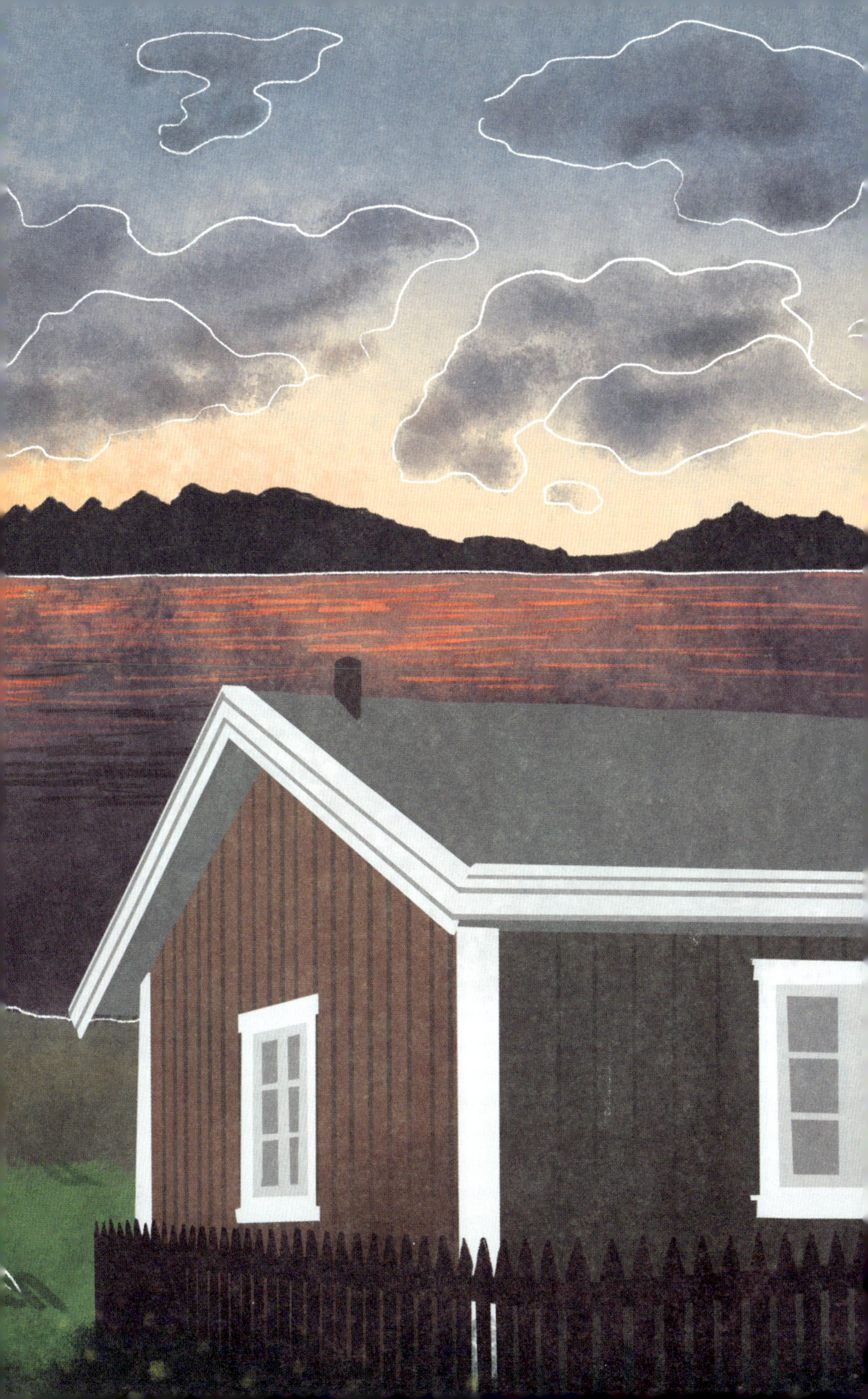

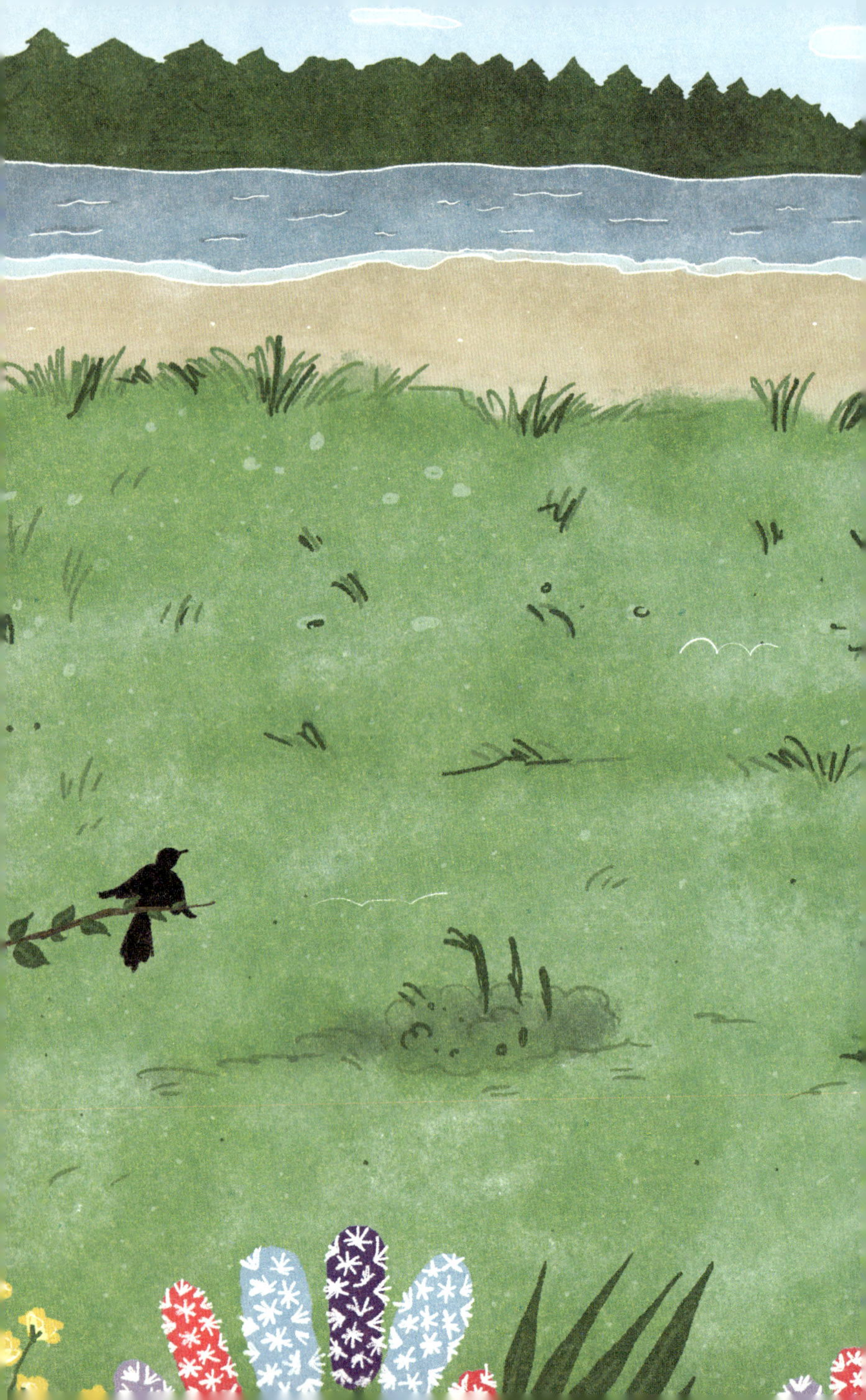

"那是种什么样的感觉?"

"就像不断在你口袋里摸索什么东西一样。一开始,你只是丢了一件小东西,随后东西越来越大。一开始,你只是忘了钥匙,最后你把人也忘了。"

"你害怕吗?"

"有一点儿,你呢?"

"有一点儿。"男孩承认。

爷爷笑了。

"害怕能让熊熊都躲开。"

诺亚的脸倚靠在爷爷的锁骨上。

"当你忘了一个人的时候,你忘了自己忘了这件事吗?"

"没有,有时候我知道自己忘了,而这是最糟糕的一种遗忘,就像被困在一场暴风雨里一样。于是我更努力地强迫自己回想起来,而这让这座广场变得地动山摇。"

"这就是为什么你会这么疲惫?"

"是的,有时候,就像是我在一张沙发上睡着了,明明那里是明亮的,醒来的时候却一片漆黑,我要花好几秒才明白自己身在何处。我深陷在太空之中,眨着眼睛,揉

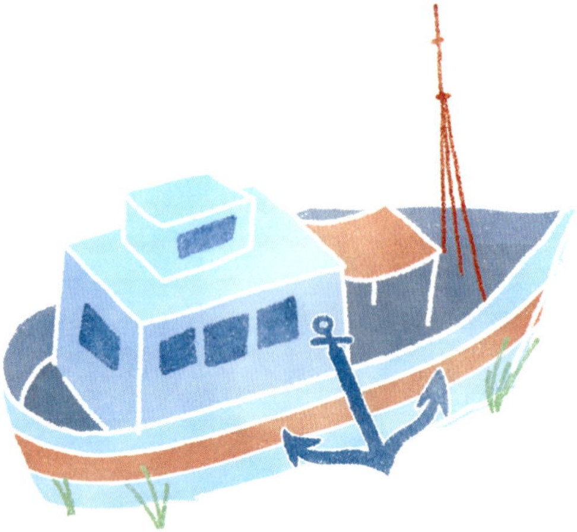

着双眼，让我的大脑多运转几下，努力回想我是谁，我在哪儿，我要怎么回家。每个清晨，回家的路都越来越长，从太空到家的路。我航行在一片平静的湖上，诺亚诺亚。"

"那太可怕了。"男孩说。

"是的，非常非常非常可怕。出于某些原因，地点和方向是最先消失的，起初你忘了你要去哪儿，接着你忘了你去过哪儿，最后你忘了你在哪儿……或者，还以另一种方式……我……我的医生说了什么，我去医生那儿，他说了些什么，或者我说了些什么。我说：'医生，我……'"

他揉着太阳穴，越来越用力。广场开始晃动起来。

"没关系。"男孩轻轻说。

"对不起，诺亚诺亚。"

男孩摩挲着他的手臂，耸了耸肩。

"别担心，我会给你一个气球，爷爷。当你迷失在太空里，你还有一个气球。"

"气球并不能阻止我继续消失，诺亚诺亚。"爷爷叹气。

"我知道，但是我会在你生日那天给你的，当作一个礼物。"

"听上去又是无用的礼物。"爷爷微笑。

男孩点点头。

"要是你一直拿着气球,那么在你将要进入太空之前,你就会知道有人曾送过你一个气球,而这是最无用的一个礼物,因为很明显一个人在太空并不需要一个气球。这会让你开心的。"

爷爷闭上眼睛,将头埋在男孩的头发里低语。

"从未有人送过我气球,这会是我得到过的最好的礼物。"

湖面上波光粼粼,爷儿俩摆动着双脚,裤腿在微风中晃来晃去。湖水和阳光的气息弥漫在长椅四周,并不是每个人都知道湖水和阳光是有味道的,但他们知道。只有当你远离其他所有的味道之后,你才会闻到它们的气息。你得坐在一艘小船里,无比放松地躺着,思想神游天外。小湖和思想在这一点上很类似,都需要花时间在其中遨游。爷爷靠着诺亚,呼出一口气,就像人们准备睡长长的一觉之前呼气一样。爷爷和诺亚,一个渐渐变大,另一个却越来越小,而岁月让他们在中间相逢。男孩指着广场另一头的路,路中间挡着一排栅栏和一块大大的警告牌。

"那里发生什么事了,爷爷?"

爷爷将头靠在诺亚的锁骨上，眨了眨眼睛。

"哦，那条路……我想它……它被封锁了。你奶奶去世的时候，那条路被雨水冲垮了。现在再去回想有点儿危险了，诺亚诺亚。"

"那条路会通向哪儿？"

"那是条捷径小路。每个早上，我在那里醒来，就会走那条路，花不了多少时间我就能回到家里了。"爷爷含糊地说，揉着他的额头。

男孩还想问点儿什么，但爷爷阻止了他。

"多跟我讲讲学校里的事，诺亚诺亚。"

诺亚耸耸肩。

"我们很少做算术，不过我们要写很多作文。"

"总是这样，明明是学校，却不准孩子学习。"

"而且我也不喜欢音乐课。爸爸想教我弹吉他，可我不会。"

"别担心，像我们这样的人会其他不同的音乐，诺亚诺亚。"

"而且我们总是在写作文！有一次，老师想让我们写下自己对生活意义的思考。"

"那你写了什么呢?"

"陪伴。"

爷爷闭上眼睛。

"这是我听到的最好的答案。"

"老师说我必须写得再长一些。"

"所以你怎么做的?"

"我写:陪伴,还有冰激凌。"

爷爷思索了那么一会儿,然后他问:"什么口味的冰激凌?"

诺亚微笑了,能被理解的感觉实在太好了。

他和女孩走在一条路上,他们重返青春了。他想起了初次遇见她的时刻,他尽量把那些画面藏好,不想让它们被大雨冲刷干净。他们那时才十六岁,那个清晨,天上下着快乐的雪花,它们像肥皂泡泡一样轻盈,落在人们冰凉的脸颊上,温柔地想要唤醒它们深爱的人。她站在他的面前,一月的雪花落在她的发间,而他一片茫然。在他的生活里,她是第一个他弄不明白的人,而在那之后,他每分每秒都想弄懂她。

"和你在一起，我才知道自己是谁。你就是我的捷径。"他向她吐露。

"哪怕我自己从来就没有方向感？"她笑了。

"死亡真不公平。"

"不，死亡是一声声缓慢的鼓点，每敲一声，它就会算一次。而我们却不能跟它讨价还价，争取更多的时间。"

"很美的说法，我的爱人。"

"这是我听别人说的。"

他们的笑声在彼此的胸膛里回响着。他接着说：

"我想念我们所有最平淡无奇的日常。阳台上的早餐，花床里的种子。"

她深呼一口气，回答：

"我想念黎明，想念日出在水底愤怒跺脚的样子，它越来越挫败，越来越焦躁，直到再也没有什么能阻止它。我想念它刚刚露出湖面时的光芒，抵达码头边的石头，最终上岸。它温暖的光辉照射在花园里，照射在我们的房子里，让我们掀开被子，开始崭新的一天。我也想念你，亲爱的你，还在睡觉的你，想念在那儿的你。"

"我们过着非凡的平凡生活。"

"是平凡的非凡生活。"

她笑了。垂暮的双眼,崭新的阳光,他还记得他们相爱的感觉是怎样的。那时,那场雨还没有降临。

他们在那条小路上翩翩起舞,直到夜幕降临。

人们在广场上来来回回,一个面容模糊的男人踩到了龙的脚,飞龙在斥责着他。一个男孩在树下弹着吉他,音调忧伤,爷爷跟着曲子轻轻哼着。一个年轻的女人赤脚走过广场,停在龙的身旁,伸手抚摩它。忽然,她的手掌在她红色外套的口袋里摸索到了什么,像是她花了很长很长时间在寻找的一样东西。她抬起头,盯着诺亚,欢笑着向他挥手,像是他帮她找到了一般,然后她告诉他不必找了,因为她已经找到了它,一切都好。有那么一瞬间,他看清了她的脸庞,她有一双奶奶的眼睛,男孩眨了眨眼,接着她就消失不见了。

"她好像……"男孩低声说。

"我知道。"爷爷点点头,他的手在自己的口袋里不安地来回摸索,然后他又举起手,指尖按压着太阳穴,像是按压装着葡萄干的盒子一样,仿佛想把里面凝结在一起的记忆松开。

"我……她……那是你的奶奶。她曾经很年轻,你永远不会见到她年轻时的模样。她有着……她有着我在人们身上见过的最为强烈的情感。每当她生气了,她能吓走一个酒吧里的所有男人,每当她快乐的时候……你无法抵抗,诺亚诺亚,她就是自然之力。我的一切都来自她,她就是我的'宇宙大爆炸'。"

"你是怎么和她相爱的?"男孩问。

爷爷的一只手放在自己的膝盖上,另一只手放在男孩的膝盖上。

"她在我的心里迷失了,我想,她找不到出来的路。你奶奶的方向感特别糟糕,她还能在自动扶梯上迷路。"

他的笑声传来,清脆爆裂,像是一块干燥的木头在他胃里燃烧,浓烟飘散出来。他伸出一只胳膊搂着男孩。

"在我的一生中,我从未问过自己,我是怎么和她相爱的,诺亚诺亚。或者还有别的原因。"

男孩看着地上的钥匙,看着广场和喷泉。他抬头仰望太空,就像他伸出手指就能触碰到它。它是柔软的。他和爷爷出去钓鱼的时候,他们偶尔会躺在船底,闭上眼睛,

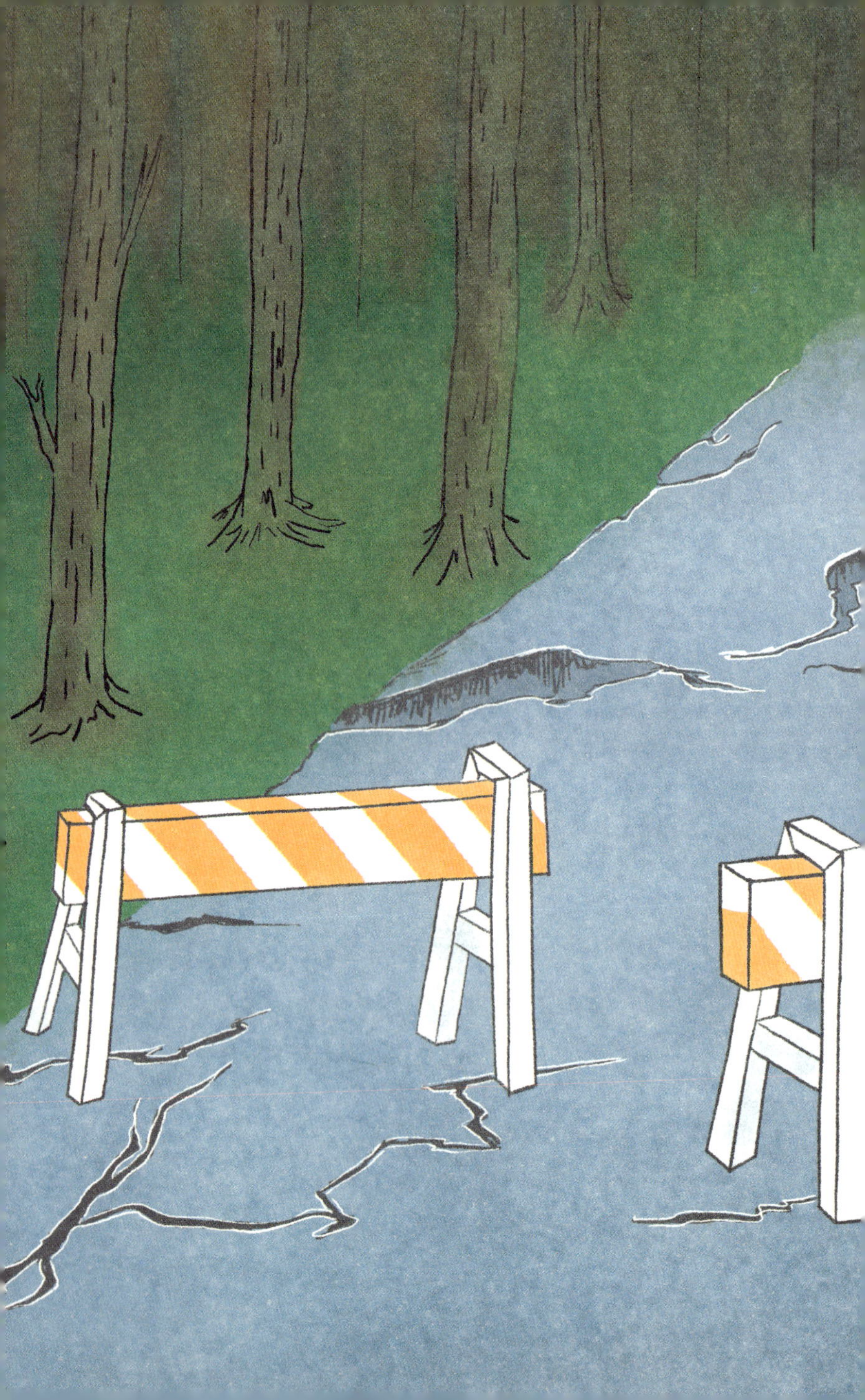

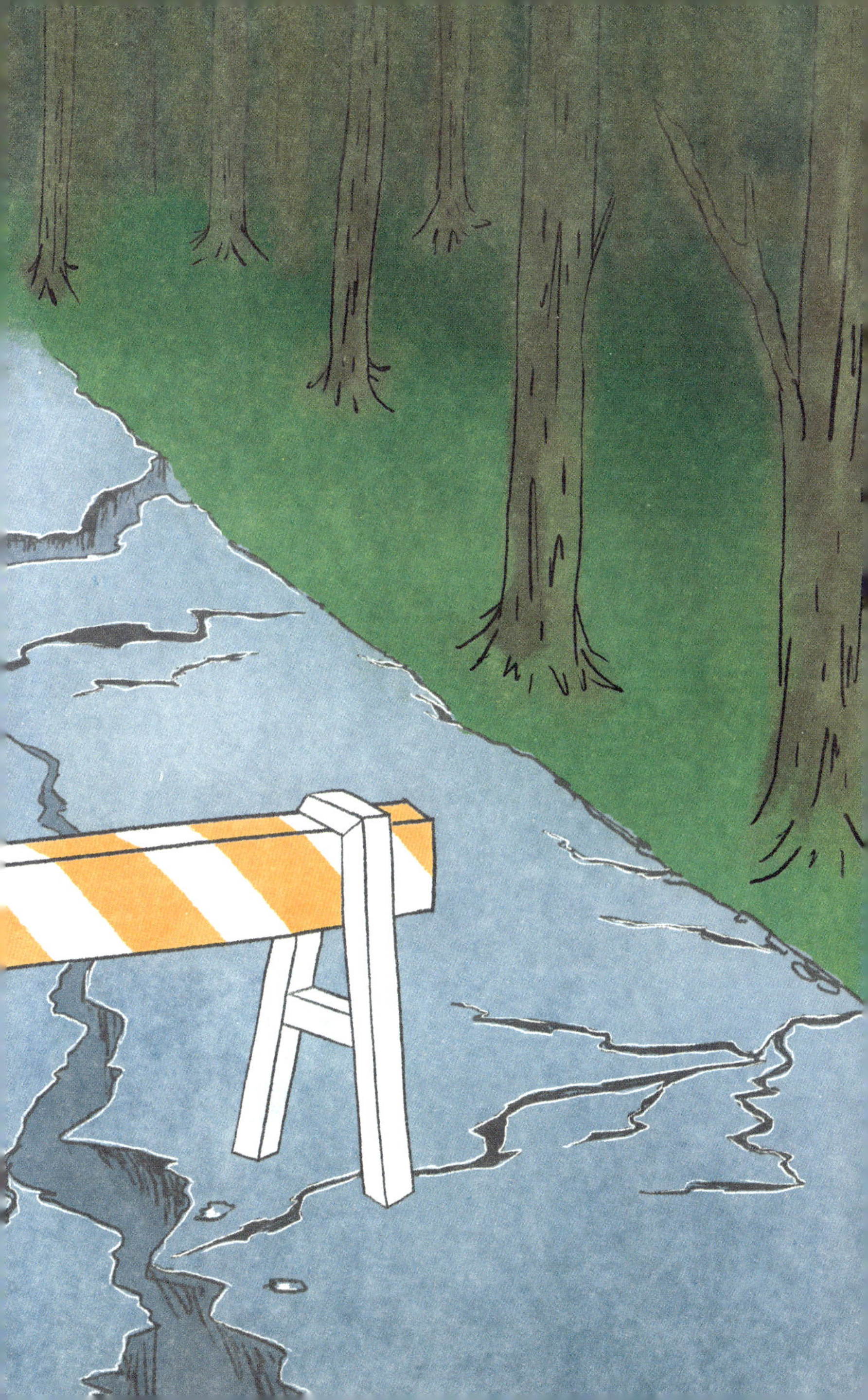

几个小时里谁也不跟谁说一句话。奶奶还在的时候，她总是待在家里，别人问她她丈夫和孙子跑哪儿去了，她就说："去太空了。"

它是属于他们的。

那是十二月的一个清晨，她去世了。整个房子里都弥漫着风信子的芳香，男孩哭了一整天。那个晚上，男孩和爷爷肩并肩躺在花园的雪地里，仰望星辰。他们一起为奶奶歌唱，也为他们自己歌唱，为太空歌唱。从那以后，他们几乎每晚都会这么做。她是属于他们的。

"你害怕你会忘掉她吗？"男孩问。

爷爷点了点头。

"很害怕。"

"或者你只需忘了她的葬礼。"男孩这么建议。

男孩可以想象他自己忘了葬礼，所有的葬礼。但爷爷却摇了摇头。

"如果我忘了葬礼，我也就忘了为什么我无法忘掉她。"

"听上去有点儿乱哦。"

"生活有时候就是这样。"

"奶奶信仰上帝，但你却不信仰。如果你死了，你还会去天堂吗?"

"只有我错了,我才会去天堂。"

男孩咬了咬嘴唇,向他承诺:

"等你忘了,爷爷,我会跟你说说她的。每天早晨,我要做的第一件事就是跟你说说她。"

爷爷握住他的手臂。

"告诉我我们曾跳过舞,诺亚诺亚。告诉我那就是相爱的感觉,就像在你心里,连你自己也装不下了。"

"我答应你。"

"还有,告诉我她很讨厌香菜,告诉我我曾告诉过餐厅里的服务生她有很严重的过敏,当他们质疑真的有人会对香菜过敏时,我就说:'相信我,她真的对香菜严重过敏,要是你们给她的食物里放了香菜,你们会死的!'她说她觉得这一点儿也不好笑,但她在以为我没有看她的时候笑了。"

"她以前说过,比起香草,香菜简直就是责罚。"诺亚笑了。

爷爷点点头,向着树梢眨了眨眼。在一片叶子落下的时间里,他深吸一口气,然后他用额头抵着男孩的额头，说：

"诺亚诺亚，答应我一件事，最后一件事：一旦你能完美地告别了，你就要离开我，别再回头，去过你自己的生活。想念一个仍旧还在的人，真是太可怕了。"

男孩花了很长一段时间思考，接着他说："你的大脑虽然病了，但好处之一却是你能很好地保守秘密。因为你是爷爷，所以这是件好事。"

爷爷点点头。

"是的，是的……那是什么秘密？"他俩都笑了。

"我想你不用因为忘了我而害怕。"思索一阵后，男孩说。

"不害怕？"

男孩把嘴凑到他的耳边：

"不用怕，如果你忘了我，那么你就有机会能重新认识我。你会很喜欢的，因为我是个很棒的人，很值得去认识。"

爷爷笑了，广场震动起来。他知道没有比这更好的祝福了。

他们坐在草地上，他和她。

"泰德很生我的气，我的爱人。"爷爷说。

"他没有生你的气，他只是生宇宙的气。他生气是因为你的敌人把他打得落花流水。"

"宇宙如此之大，要是生它的气，那就是无尽的愤怒了。我倒希望他……"

"他更像你一些？"

"少一些，少像我一些，少一点儿愤怒。"

"他是的，只是更加悲伤一些。你还记得在他还小的时候，曾经问你人们为什么要去太空吗？"

"记得，我告诉他人类天生就有冒险精神，我们渴望去探索和发现，那是我们的本性。"

"但是你能看出他很害怕，所以你又说：'泰德，我们不去太空，是因为我们害怕外星人。我们去太空呢，是因为我们害怕自己太孤独。在这茫茫宇宙中孤身一人，实在是太可怕了。'"

"我说过吗？我居然这么聪明。"

"你可能是从别人那里听来的。"

"可能吧。"

"也许泰德现在在跟诺亚说同样的话。"

"诺亚从不害怕太空。"

"那是因为诺亚像我，他信仰上帝。"

老人躺在草地上，朝着树林微笑。她站了起来，穿过树篱，沿着船边走着，若有所思地轻抚着它。

"别忘了在锚下多垫些石头，诺亚长得太快了。"她提醒他。

那个他曾经在里面工作了很多年的船舱，此刻在薄暮中显得如此渺小，即便它的空间足以盛放他所有庞大的想法。那几盏灯还在船外，他曾把它们乱七八糟地系在外面，就是怕诺亚从噩梦中醒来想要找他爷爷，这几盏灯就能帮他找到爷爷了。灯泡五颜六色，绿的、黄的、紫的，像是爷爷急着要上厕所，就胡乱地把它们挂上去了。这样，诺亚就能在看到它们的时候哈哈大笑。要是你在笑，那么你在穿过一座黑暗的花园时就不会害怕了。

她躺在他的身旁，靠得那么近。她叹息着。

"我们在这里创造了我们的生活，创造了一切。在那条路上，你还教过泰德骑自行车。"

他抿着嘴唇，坦白道："泰德是自学的，就像我叫他别再碰吉他了，好好去做功课，而他却自己学会了弹吉他。"

"你太忙了。"她轻声说，每个字里都盛满了愧疚，因为她自己也同样很自责。

"现在泰德也很忙。"他说。

"但是这个宇宙给了你们诺亚，他是你俩之间的桥梁。这就是我们为什么如此爱我们的孙子，因为只有这样我们才能向我们的孩子致以歉意。"

"那我们要怎么做，才能让孩子们不因为这件事而讨厌我们呢？"

"我们做不到的，那不是我们的工作。"

他口中的那句话如鲠在喉。

"所有人都好奇你是怎么忍受我的，我的爱人。有时候我也会很好奇。"

她咯咯地笑了，他是多么想念她的笑声。那笑声就像是从她脚底飞快地迸发出来的。

"你是我遇到的第一个知道怎么跳舞的男孩。我想，也许我最好抓住机会。谁知道这样的男孩会什么时候再出现。"

"我很抱歉，因为香菜的事。"

"没有，你才不觉得抱歉呢。"

"真的，我很抱歉。"

黑暗中，她悄悄松开了他的手，但她的声音仍在他的耳畔。

"别忘了在锚底下多垫几块石头，再问问泰德吉他的事。"

"现在太晚了。"

她的笑声在他脑海里回响着。

"亲爱的顽固的你啊，问你儿子他热爱的事物，永远也不会晚的。"

雨开始落下来，他向她呼喊的最后一句话是他也希望他错了。他多么、多么、多么希望他错了，这样，她就能在天堂继续和他争吵了。

一个男孩和他爸爸沿着走廊走着。爸爸温柔地牵着他的手。

"害怕很正常，诺亚，你不必感到羞愧。"他不断地说。

"我知道，爸爸，别担心。"诺亚说着，两人滑了一跤，诺亚提了提裤子。

"裤子有一点儿大了,不过这是他们最小的尺码了。等我们回到家里,我把它再裁剪一下让它更适合你。"爸爸向他保证。

"爷爷很痛苦吗?"诺亚很想知道。

"没有,不用担心,只是在船里摔了一跤的时候,他磕到了头。看着很惨,但不怎么痛,诺亚。"

"我是说在心里,心里的伤口还疼吗?"

爸爸用鼻子深呼吸着,他闭上眼睛,他的步伐慢了下来。

"这很难解释,诺亚。"

诺亚点点头,用力地牵着他的手。

"别害怕,爸爸,它能让熊熊都躲开。"

"什么能让熊熊都躲开?"

"我在救护车里尿裤子了,尿臊气能让熊熊都躲开。救护车里再也不会有熊熊了。"

爸爸的笑声像隆隆的雷声,诺亚很喜欢听。那双大大的手轻轻地牵着他小小的手。

"我们只需和你爷爷在一起的时候小心一点儿,明白吗?他的大脑……诺亚,有时候大脑会比我们以前运转得

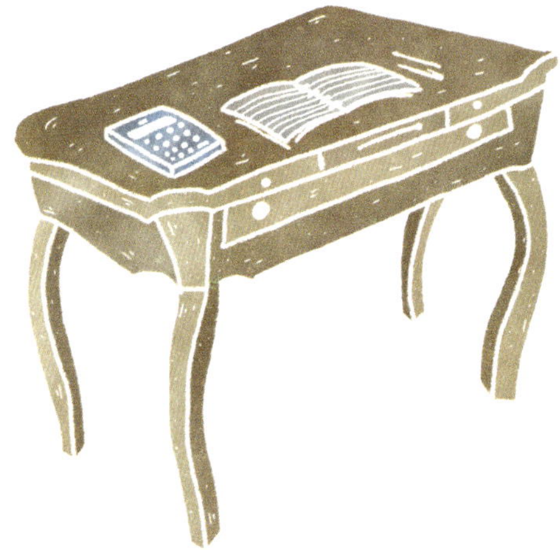

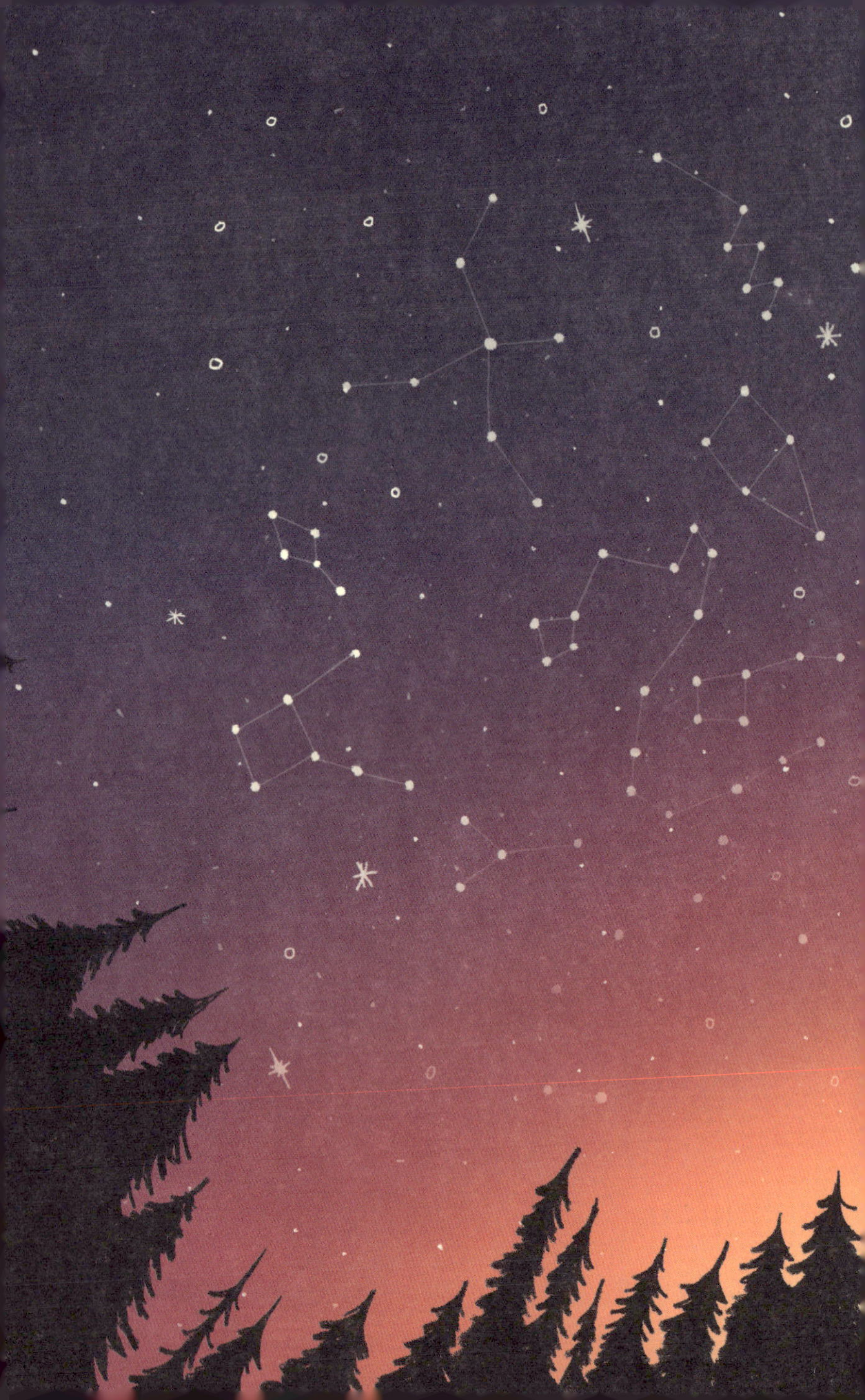

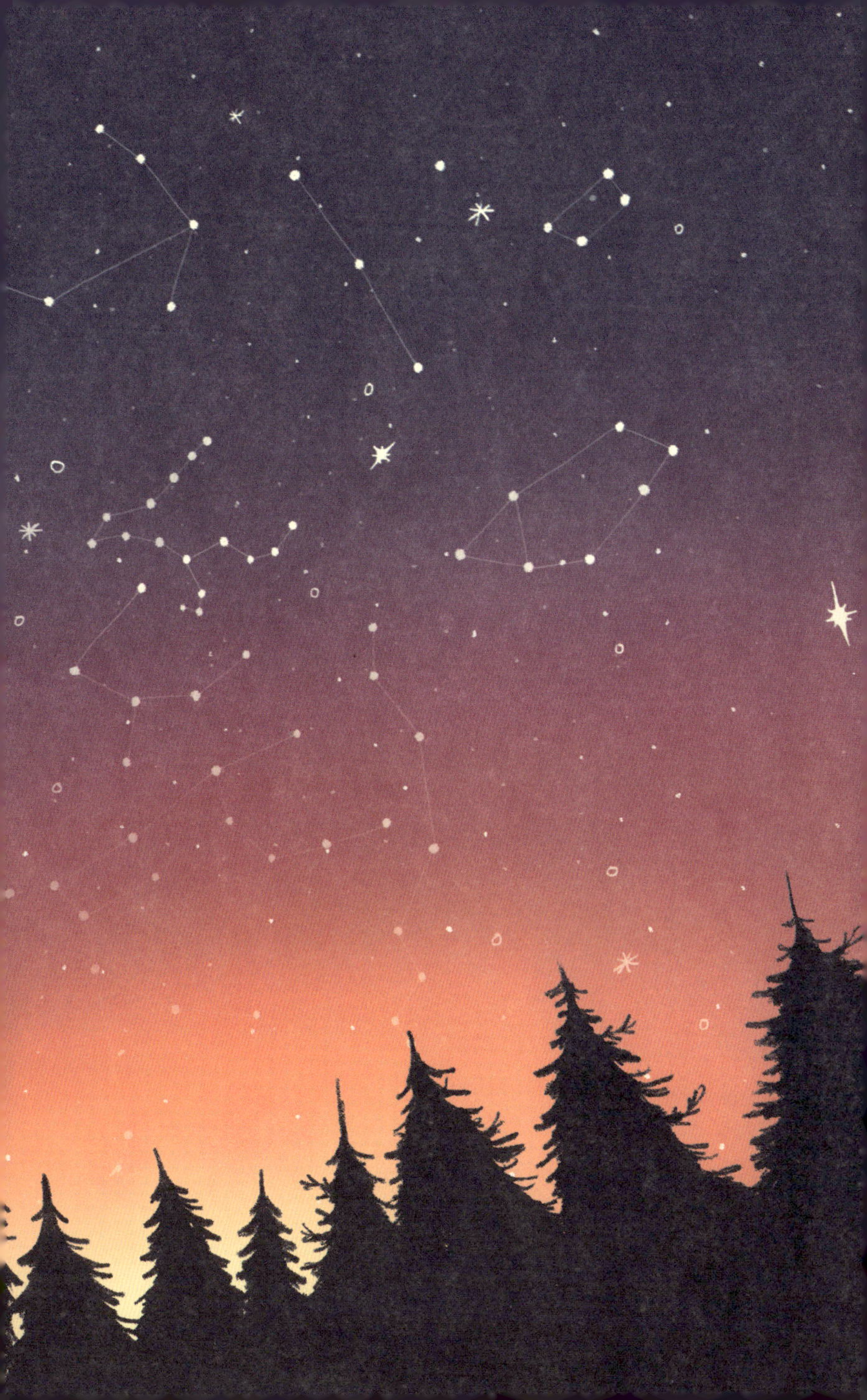

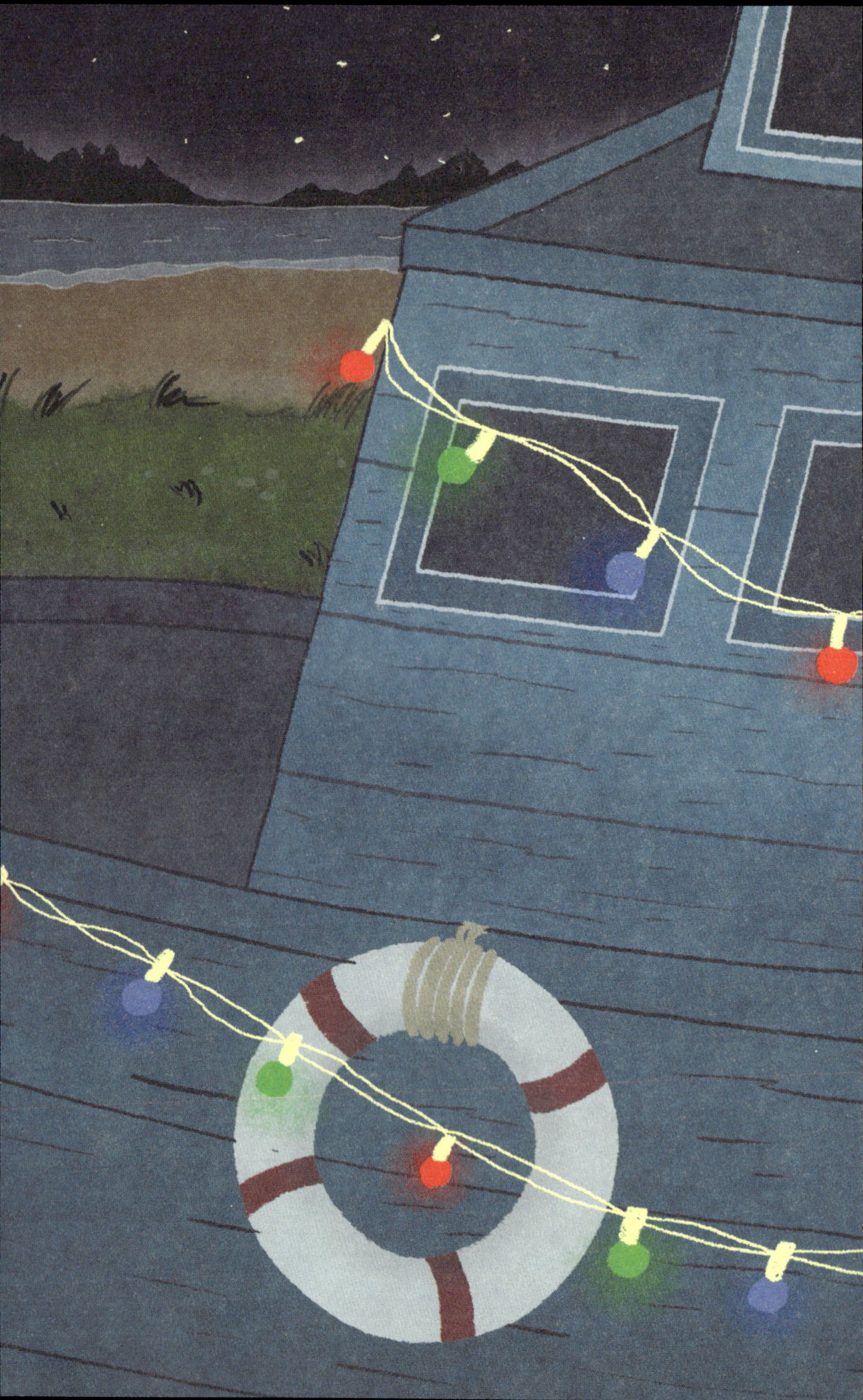

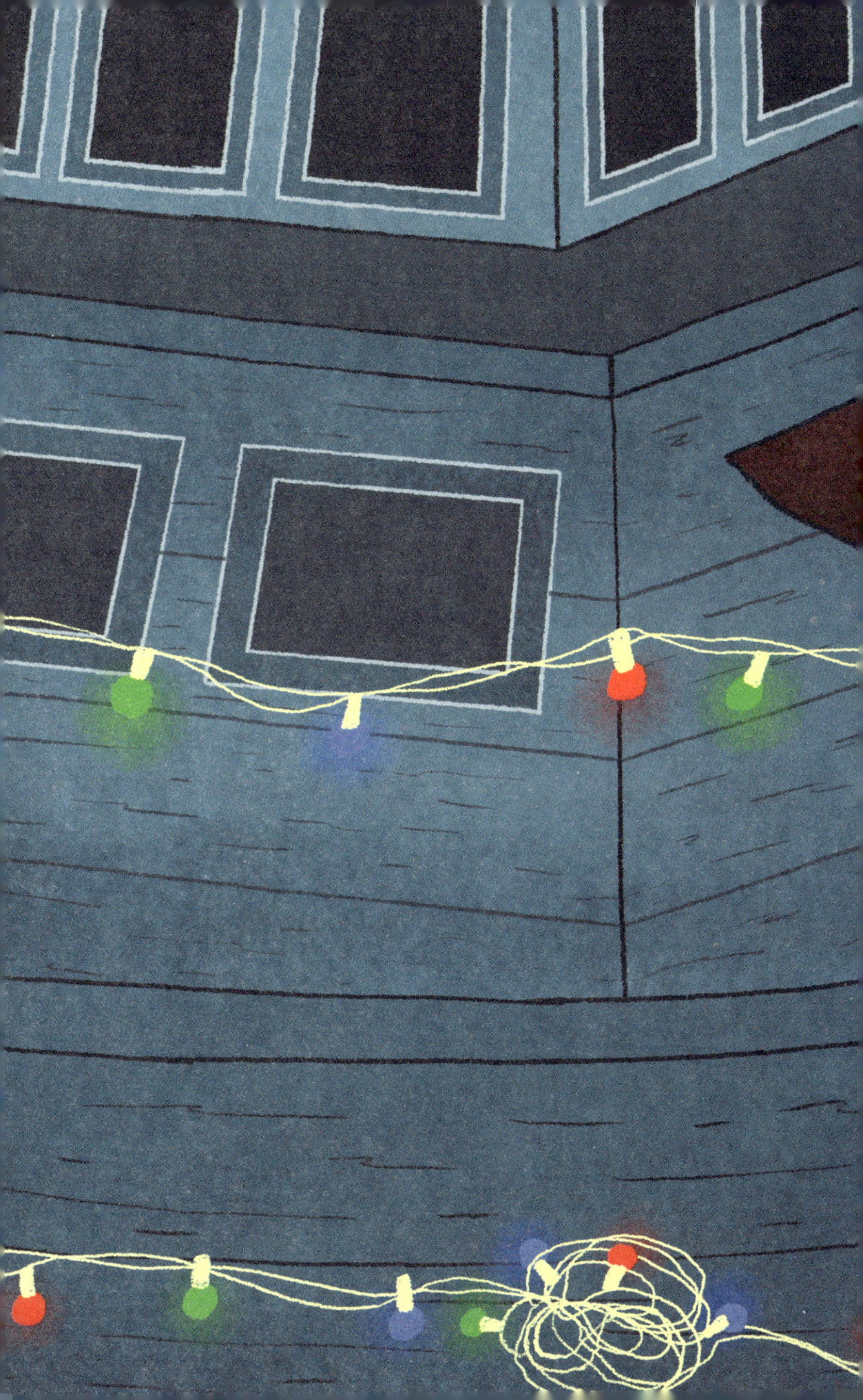

慢一些。爷爷的大脑比他过去要运转得慢一些。"

"是的，现在，每个清晨回家的路都越来越长了。"

爸爸蹲下来拥抱着他。

"我可爱的、聪慧的小儿子，我对你的爱，诺亚，连天空也容纳不下。"

"我们能做些什么来帮助爷爷呀？"

爸爸的眼泪在男孩的运动衫上干涸了。

"我们可以陪他走走路，我们可以陪伴着他。"

他们乘坐电梯来到了医院的停车场，牵着手朝车走去，去取他们的绿色帐篷。

泰德和他的爸爸又在争论了。泰德恳求他坐下来，爸爸却怒吼着："我今天没有时间教你骑自行车，泰德！我告诉过你，我得工作！"

"没事，爸爸，好的。"

"看在上帝的分上，我想要我的香烟！告诉我，你把我的香烟藏到哪里去了？！"爸爸咆哮道。

"你几年前就戒烟了。"泰德说。

"该死的，你怎么知道的？"

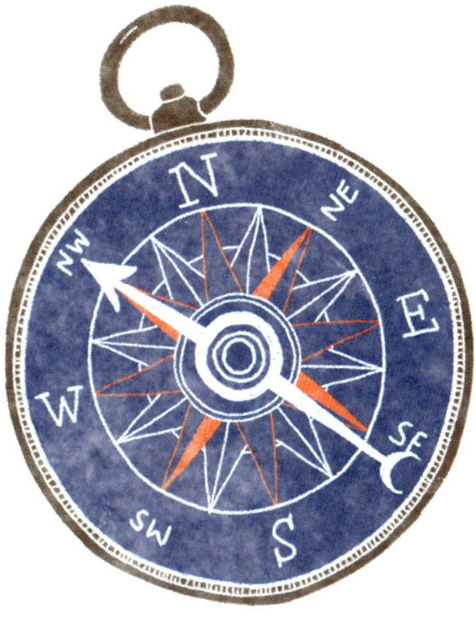
N
NE
E
SE
S
SW
W
NW

"我之所以知道是因为你在我出生的时候就戒掉了，爸爸。"

他们彼此注视着，喘着气。吸气，呼气，吸气，呼气。跟宇宙生气，那将会是无尽的怒火。

"我……它……"爷爷咕哝着。

泰德大大的手按着他瘦弱的肩膀，爷爷摸了摸他的胡须。

"你长这么大了啊，泰德泰德。"

"爸爸，听我说，诺亚现在在这里。他会和你坐在一起，我要去车里拿点儿东西。"

爷爷点了点头，把他的额头靠在了泰德的额头上。

"我们得赶快回家了，我的儿子。你的妈妈还在等我们，我敢肯定，她现在很担心。"

泰德咬住了下唇。

"好的，爸爸，很快。真的、真的很快。"

"你现在多高了，泰德泰德？"

"六尺一[1]，爸爸。"

---

[1] 约1.85米。

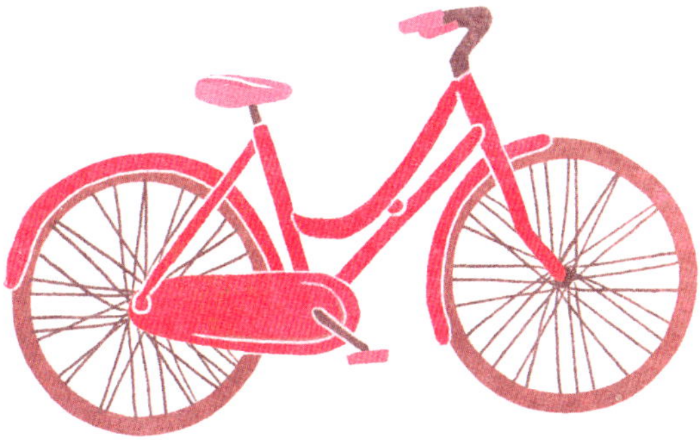

"等我们回到家，我们要在锚下多垫几块石头。"

爷爷问他是否带着吉他的时候，泰德已经快走到了门边。

在生命的尽头，有一间病房。有人在病房中央搭了一个绿色帐篷，一个人在里面醒了过来，呼吸急促，惊恐不安，不知自己身在何处。一个年轻的男人坐在他的身旁,轻声说：

"别怕。"

那个人从睡袋里坐了起来，环抱着自己颤抖的膝盖，哭泣着。

"别害怕。"年轻的男人不断地说。

一个气球在帐篷顶上弹跳着，气球线的一头系在了他的指尖上。

"我不知道你是谁。"他低声说。年轻的男人拍了拍他的前臂。

"我是诺亚，你是我的爷爷。你在你家外面的那条路上教过我骑自行车，你很爱我的奶奶，所以在你心里连你自己也装不下了。她很讨厌香菜，却忍受得了你。你发过誓说永远不会戒烟，但当你成为一个父亲时，你却戒烟了。

你去过外太空,因为你天生就是探险家。有一次你去看医生,你说:'医生,医生,我在两个地方弄伤了我的胳膊!'然后医生就告诉你不要再去那两个地方了。"

爷爷微笑着,嘴唇也不再颤动。诺亚把系着气球的线放在了他的手心里,给他看他是怎么握着线的另一头的。

"我们在一个湖边的帐篷里睡觉呢,这个帐篷是我们以前在湖边睡觉时常用的,爷爷,你还记得吗?如果你把线系在手腕上,你就能在入睡的时候还拿着这个气球。要是你害怕了,你只要拉一拉这个气球,我就会带你回来。每一次我都会的。"

爷爷缓缓地点着头,他惊讶地轻抚着诺亚的脸颊。

"你变了,诺亚诺亚,学校的生活怎么样?现在的老师好一点儿了吗?"

"是的,爷爷,老师们变好了。如今,我也是一名老师了。老师们现在都特别棒。"

"很好,很好,诺亚诺亚,伟大的大脑绝不应该被禁锢在地球上。"爷爷闭上眼睛,轻声说。

病房外,太空正在歌唱。泰德在弹着吉他,爷爷应和着音乐哼唱着。宇宙很浩大,生活同样很漫长。诺亚抚摩着女儿的头发，那个女孩还在睡袋里面朝着他熟睡着，没有醒来。她不喜欢数学，反而喜欢文字和乐器，就像她的爷爷一样。很快，她的脚也能触碰到地面了。他们睡成一排，帐篷里弥漫着风信子的芬芳。他再也没有什么可害怕的了。

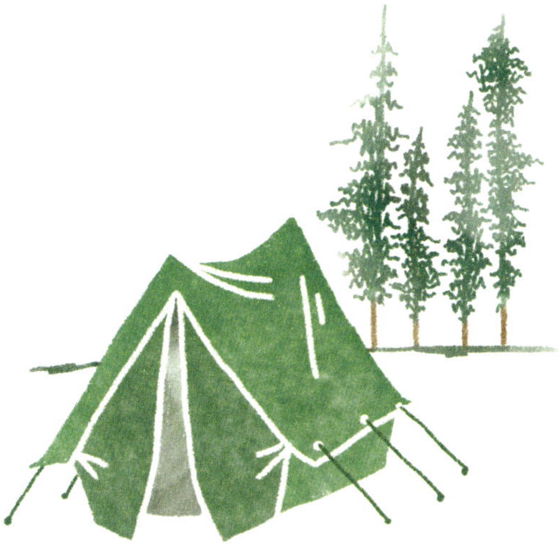

AND EVERY MORNING

THE WAY HOME

GETS LONGER AND LONGER

a novella by
Fredrik Backman

Dear Reader:

One of my idols once said, "The worst part about growing old is that I don't get any ideas anymore." Those words have never quite left me since I first heard them, because this would be my greatest fear: imagination giving up before the body does. I guess I'm not alone in this. Humans are a strange breed in the way our fear of getting old seems to be even greater than our fear of dying.

This is a story about memories and about letting go. It's a love letter and a slow farewell between a man and his grandson, and between a dad and his boy.

I never meant for you to read it, to be quite honest. I wrote it just because I was trying to sort out my own thoughts, and I'm the kind of person who needs to see what I'm thinking on paper to make sense of it. But it turned into a small tale of how I'm dealing with slowly losing the greatest minds I know, about missing someone who is still here, and how I wanted to explain it all to my children. I'm letting it go now, for what it's worth.

It's about fear and love, and how they seem to go hand in hand most of the time. Most of all, it's about time. While we still have it. Thank you for giving this story yours.

Fredrik Backman

AND EVERY MORNING
THE WAY HOME
GETS LONGER AND LONGER

There's a hospital room at the end of a life where someone, right in the middle of the floor, has pitched a green tent. A person wakes up inside it, breathless and afraid, not knowing where he is. A young man sitting next to him whispers: "Don't be scared."

Isn't that the best of all life's ages, an old man thinks as he looks at his grandchild. When a boy is just big enough to know how the world works but still young enough to refuse to accept it. Noah's feet don't touch the ground when his legs dangle over the edge of the bench, but his head reaches all the way to space, because he hasn't been alive long enough to allow anyone to keep his thoughts on Earth. His grandpa is next to him and is incredibly old, of course, so old now that people have given up and no longer nag him to start acting like an adult. So old that it's too late to grow up. It's not so bad either, that age.

The bench is in a square; Noah blinks heavily at the sunrise beyond it, newly woken. He doesn't want to admit to Grandpa that he doesn't know where they are, because this has always been their game: Noah closes his eyes and Grandpa takes him somewhere they've never been before. Sometimes the boy has to squeeze his eyes tight, tight shut while he and Grandpa change buses four times in town, and sometimes Grandpa just takes him straight into the woods behind the house by the lake. Sometimes they go in the boat, often for so long that Noah falls asleep, and once they've made it far enough Grandpa whispers "open your eyes" and gives Noah a map and a compass and the task of working out how they're going to get home. Grandpa knows he'll always manage, because there are two things in life in which Grandpa's faith is unwavering: mathematics and his grandson. A group of people calculated how to fly three men to the moon when Grandpa was young, and mathematics took them all the way there and back again. Numbers always lead people back.

But this place lacks coordinates; there are no roads out, no maps lead here.

Noah remembers that Grandpa asked him to close his eyes today. He remembers that they crept out of Grandpa's house and he knows that Grandpa took him to the lake, because the boy knows all the sounds and songs of the water, eyes open or not. He remembers damp wood underfoot as they stepped into the boat, but nothing after that. He doesn't know how he and Grandpa ended up here, on a bench in a round square. The place is strange but everything here is familiar, like someone stole all the things you grew up with and put them into the wrong house. There's a desk over there, just like the one in Grandpa's office, with a mini calculator and squared notepaper on top. Grandpa whistles gently, a sad tune, takes a quick little break to whisper: "The square got smaller overnight again."

Then he starts whistling again. Grandpa seems surprised when the boy gives him a questioning look, aware for the first time that he said those words aloud.

"Sorry, Noahnoah, I forgot that thoughts aren't silent here."

Grandpa always calls him "Noahnoah" because he likes his grandson's name twice as much as everyone else's. He puts a hand in the boy's hair, not ruffling it, just letting his fingers rest there.

"There's nothing to be afraid of, Noahnoah."

Hyacinths are blooming beneath the bench, a million tiny purple arms reaching up from the stalks to embrace the rays of sunlight. The boy recognizes the flowers, they're Grandma's, they smell like Christmas. For other children maybe that scent would be ginger biscuits and mulled wine, but if you've ever had a Grandma who loved things that grew then Christmas will always smell like hyacinths. There are shards of glass and keys glittering between the flowers, like someone had been keeping them safe in a big jar but then fell over and dropped it.

"What are all those keys for?" the boy asks.

"Which keys?" asks Grandpa.

The old man's eyes are strangely empty now. He raps his temples in frustration. The boy opens his mouth to say something, but stops himself when he sees that. He sits quietly instead and does what Grandpa taught him to do if he gets lost: take in his surroundings, look for landmarks and clues. The bench is surrounded by trees, because Grandpa loves trees, because trees don't give a damn what people think. Silhouettes of birds lift up from them, spread out across the heavens, and rest confidently on the winds. A dragon is crossing the square, green and sleepy, and a penguin with small chocolate-colored handprints on its stomach is sleeping in one corner. A soft owl with only one eye is sitting next to it. Noah recognizes them too; they used to be his. Grandpa gave him the dragon when he had just been born, because Grandma said it wasn't suitable to give newborn children dragons as cuddly toys and Grandpa said he didn't want a suitable grandson.

People are walking around the square, but they're blurry. When the boy tries to focus on their outlines they slip from his eyes like light through venetian blinds. One of them stops and waves to Grandpa. Grandpa waves back, tries to look confident.

"Who's that?" the boy asks.

"That's…I…I can't remember, Noahnoah. It was so long ago…I think…"

He falls silent, hesitates, and searches for something in his pockets.

"You haven't given me a map and a compass today, nothing to count on, I don't know how I'm meant to find the way home, Grandpa." Noah whispers.

"I'm afraid those things won't help us here, Noahnoah."

"Where are we, Grandpa?"

Then Grandpa starts to cry, silently and tearlessly, so that his grandson won't realize.

"It's hard to explain, Noahnoah. It's so incredibly, incredibly hard to explain."

The girl is standing in front of him and smells like hyacinths, like she's never been anywhere else. Her hair is old but the wind in it is new, and he still remembers what it felt like to fall in love; that's the last memory to abandon him. Falling in love with her meant having no room in his own body. That was why he danced.

"We had too little time." he says.

She shakes her head.

"We had an eternity. Children and grandchildren."

"I only had you for the blink of an eye." he says.

She laughs.

"You had me an entire lifetime. All of mine."

"That wasn't enough."

She kisses his wrist; her chin rests in his fingers.

"No."

They walk slowly along a road he thinks he has walked before, not remembering where it leads. His hand is wrapped safely around hers and they're sixteen again, no shaking fingers, no aching hearts. His chest tells him he could run to the horizon, but one breath passes and his lungs won't obey him anymore. She stops, waits patiently beneath the weight of his arm, and she's old now, like the day before she left him. He whispers into her eyelid: "I don't know how to explain it to Noah."

"I know." she says and her breath sings against his neck.

"He's so big now, I wish you could see him."

"I do, I do."

"I miss you, my love."

"I'm still with you, darling difficult you."

"But only in my memories now. Only here."

"That doesn't matter. This was always my favorite part of you."

"I've filled the square. It got smaller overnight again."

"I know, I know."

Then she dabs his forehead with a soft handkerchief, making small red circles bloom on the material, and she admonishes him: "You're bleeding; you need to be careful when you get into the boat."

He closes his eyes.

"What do I say to Noah? How do I explain that I'm going to be leaving him even before I die?"

She takes his jaw in her hands and kisses him.

"Darling difficult husband, you should explain this to our grandson the way you've always explained everything to him: as though he was smarter than you."

He holds her close. He knows the rain will be coming soon.

Noah can see that Grandpa is ashamed the minute he says it's hard to explain, because Grandpa never says that to Noah. All other adults do, Noah's dad does it every day, but not Grandpa.

"I don't mean it would be hard for you to understand, Noahnoah. I mean it's hard for me to understand." the old man apologizes.

"You're bleeding!" the boy cries.

Grandpa's fingers fumble across his forehead. A single drop of blood is teetering on the edge of a deep gash in his skin, right above his eyebrow, sitting there fighting gravity. Eventually it falls, onto Grandpa's shirt, and two more drops immediately do the same, just like when children leap into the sea from a jetty, one has to be brave enough to go first before the others will follow.

"Yes...yes, I suppose I am, I must've...fallen." Grandpa broods as though that should have been a thought too.

But there are no silent thoughts here. The boy's eyes widen.

"Wait, you...you fell in the boat. I remember now! That's how you hurt yourself, I shouted for Dad!"

"Dad?" Grandpa repeats.

"Yeah, don't be scared Grandpa, Dad's coming to get us soon!" Noah promises as he pats Grandpa on the forearm, soothing him with a degree of experience far beyond what a boy his age should have.

Grandpa's pupils bounce anxiously, so the boy resolutely continues: "Do you remember what you always said when we went fishing on the island and slept in the tent? There's nothing wrong with being a bit scared, you said, because if you wet yourself it'll keep the bears away!"

Grandpa blinks tightly, as though even Noah's outline has gotten blurry, but then the old man nods several times, his eyes clearer.

"Yes! Yes, so I did, Noahnoah, I said that, didn't I? When we were fishing. Oh, darling Noahnoah, you've grown so big. So very big. How is school?"

Noah steadies his voice, tries to swallow the trembling of his vocal cords as his heart pounds in alarm.

"It's fine. I'm top of the class in math. Just keep calm, Grandpa, Dad's going to come and get us soon."

Grandpa's hand rests on the boy's shoulder.

"That's good, Noahnoah, that's good. Mathematics will always lead you home."

The boy is terrified now, but knows better than to let Grandpa see that, so he shouts: "Three point one four one!"

"Five nine two," Grandpa immediately replies.

"Six five three." the boy reels off.

"Five eight nine." Grandpa laughs.

That's another of Grandpa's favorite games, reciting the decimals of pi, the mathematical constant which is the key to calculating the size of a circle. Grandpa loves the magic of it, those key numbers which unlock secrets, open up the entire universe to us. He knows more than two hundred decimals of it by heart; the boy's record is half that. Grandpa always says that the years will allow them to meet in the middle, when the boy's thoughts expand and Grandpa's contract.

"Seven." says the boy.

"Nine." Grandpa whispers.

The boy squeezes his rough palm, and Grandpa sees that he is afraid, so the old man says: "Have I ever told you about the time I went to the doctor, Noahnoah? I said, 'Doctor, Doctor, I've broken my arm in two places!' and the doctor replied, 'Then I'd advise you to stop going there!'"

The boy blinks, things are becoming increasingly blurred.

"You've told that one before, Grandpa. It's your favorite joke."

"Oh." Grandpa whispers, ashamed.

The square is a perfect circle. The wind fights in the treetops; the leaves move in a hundred dialects of green. Grandpa has always loved this time of year. Warm winds wander through the arms of the hyacinths and small drops of blood dry on his forehead. Noah holds his fingers there and asks: "Where are we, Grandpa? Why are my stuffed animals here in the square? What happened when you fell in the boat?"

And then Grandpa's tears leave his eyelashes.

"We're in my brain, Noahnoah. And it got smaller overnight again."

Ted and his dad are in a garden. It smells like hyacinths.

"How is school?" the dad asks gruffly.

He always asks that and Ted can never give the right answer. The dad likes numbers and the boy likes letters; they're different languages.

"I got top marks for my essay." says the boy.

"And mathematics? How are you doing in mathematics? How are words meant to guide you home if you're lost in the woods?" the dad grunts.

The boy doesn't reply; he doesn't understand numbers, or maybe the numbers don't understand him. They've never seen eye to eye, his dad and him.

The dad, still a young man, bends down and starts pulling weeds from a flower bed. When he gets back up it's dark, though he could swear only a moment had passed.

"Three point one four one." he mumbles, but the voice no longer sounds like his own.

"Dad?" says the son's voice, but different now, deeper.

"Three point one four one! It's your favorite game!" roars the dad.

"No." the son softly replies.

"It was your..." the dad starts, but the air betrays his words.

"You're bleeding, Dad." says the boy.

The dad blinks at him several times, but then shakes his head and chuckles exaggeratedly.

"Ah, it's just a graze. Have I ever told you about the time I went to the doctor? I said, 'Doctor, Doctor, I've broken my arm...' "

He falls silent.

"You're bleeding, Dad." the boy repeats patiently.

"I said, 'I've broken my arm.' Or no, wait, I said...I can't remember...it's my favorite joke, Ted. It's my favorite joke. Stop pulling at me,

I can tell my favorite bloody joke!"

The boy carefully takes hold of his hands, but they're small now.

The boy's are like spades in comparison. "Whose hands are these?" the old man pants.

"They're mine." Ted replies.

The dad shakes his head, blood runs from his forehead. Anger fills his eyes.

"Where's my boy? Where's my little boy? Answer me!"

"Sit down a minute, Dad." Ted begs.

The dad's pupils hunt the dusk around the treetops; he tries to cry out but can't remember how; his throat will only give him hissing sounds now.

"How is school, Ted? How are you doing in mathematics?"

Mathematics will always lead you home…

"You need to sit down, Dad, you're bleeding." the son begs.

He has a beard; it bristles beneath the dad's palm when he touches the boy's cheek.

"What happened?" whispers the dad.

"You fell over in the boat. I told you not to go out in the boat, Dad. It's dangerous, especially when you take No—"

The dad's eyes widen and he excitedly interrupts: "Ted? Is that you? You've changed! How is school?"

Ted breathes slowly, talks clearly: "I don't go to school anymore, Dad. I'm grown up now."

"How did your essay go?"

"Sit down now, please, Dad. Sit down."

"You look scared, Ted. Why are you scared?"

"Don't worry, Dad. I was just…I…you can't go out in the boat. I've told you a thousand times… "

They aren't in the garden anymore; they're in an odorless room with white walls. The dad lays his hand on the bearded cheek.

"Don't be scared, Ted. Do you remember when I taught you to fish? When we stayed in the tent out on the island and you had to sleep in my sleeping bag because you had a nightmare and wet yourself? Do you remember what I said to you? That it's good to wet yourself because it keeps the bears away. There's nothing wrong with being a bit scared."

When the dad sits down he lands on a soft bed, freshly made up by someone who isn't going to sleep there. This isn't his room. Ted is sitting next to him and the old man buries his nose in his son's hair.

"Do you remember, Ted? The tent on the island?"

"That wasn't me in the tent with you, Dad. It was Noah." the son whispers.

The dad lifts his head and stares at him. "Who's Noah?"

Ted gently strokes his cheek.

"Noah, Dad. My son. You stayed in the tent with Noah. I don't like fishing."

"You do! I taught you! I taught you…didn't I teach you?"

"You never had time to teach me, Dad. You were always working. But you taught Noah, you've taught him everything. He's the one who loves math, like you."

The father's fingers grope around the bed; he's looking for something in his pockets, more and more frantically. When he sees that his boy has tears in his eyes, his own gaze flees toward the corner of the room. He clenches his fists until his knuckles turn white to stop them from shaking, mutters angrily: "But what about school, Ted? Tell me how it's going at school!"

A boy and his grandpa are sitting on a bench in Grandpa's brain.

"It's such a nice brain, Grandpa." Noah says encouragingly, because Grandma always said that whenever Grandpa goes quiet, you just have to give him a compliment to get him going again.

"That's nice of you." Grandpa smiles and dries his eyes with the back of his hand.

"A bit messy though." The boy grins.

"It rained for a long time here when your Grandma died. I never quite got it back in order after that."

Noah notices that the ground beneath the bench has become muddy, but the keys and shards of glass are still there. Beyond the square is the lake, and small waves roll over it, memories of boats already passed. Noah can almost see the green tent on the island in the distance, remembers the fog which used to tenderly hug the trees like a cool sheet at dawn when they woke. Whenever Noah was scared of sleeping, Grandpa would take out a string and tie one end around his arm and the other around the boy's and promise that if Noah had nightmares he only had to pull on the string and Grandpa would wake up and bring him straight back to safety. Like a boat on a jetty. Grandpa kept his promise, every single time. Noah's legs dangle over the edge of the bench; the dragon has fallen asleep in the middle of the square, next to a fountain. There's a small group of tall buildings on the horizon on the other shore, amid the ruins of others which look like they've recently fallen down. The last ones standing are covered in blinking neon lights, strung here and there across their facades like they were taped up by someone who was either in too much of a hurry or absolutely desperate for a poo. They wink patterns through the fog, Noah realizes, forming letters. "Important!" one of the buildings twinkles. "Remember!" says another one. But on the very tallest building, the one closest to the beach, the lights say, "Pictures of Noah."

"What are those buildings, Grandpa?"

"They're archives. That's where everything is kept. All the most important things."

"Like what?"

"Everything we've done. All the photos and films and all your most unnecessary presents."

Grandpa laughs, Noah too. They always give each other unnecessary presents. Grandpa gave Noah a plastic bag full of air for Christmas and Noah gave Grandpa a sandal. For his birthday, Noah gave Grandpa a piece of chocolate he'd already eaten. That was Grandpa's favorite.

"That's a big building."

"It was a big piece of chocolate."

"Why are you holding my hand so tight, Grandpa?"

"Sorry, Noahnoah. Sorry."

The ground around the fountain in the square is covered in hard stone slabs. Someone has scrawled advanced mathematical calculations all over them in white chalk, but blurry people are rushing this way and that across them and the soles of their shoes rub away the numbers one by one until only random lines remain, carved deeply into the stones. Fossil equations. The dragon sneezes in its sleep, its nostrils send a million scraps of paper covered in handwritten messages flying across the square. A hundred elves from a book of fairy tales Grandma used to read to Noah dance around the fountain trying to catch them.

"What's on those pieces of paper?" the boy asks.

"Those are all my ideas." Grandpa replies.

"They're blowing away."

"They've been doing that for a long time."

The boy nods and wraps his fingers tightly around Grandpa's.

"Is your brain ill?"

"Who told you that?"

"Dad."

Grandpa exhales through his nose. Nods.

"We don't know, really. We know so little about how the brain works. It's like a fading star right now—do you remember what I taught you about that?"

"When a star fades it takes a long time for us to realize, as long as it takes for the last of its light to reach Earth."

Grandpa's chin trembles. He often reminds Noah that the universe is over thirteen billion years old. Grandma always used to mutter: "And you're still in such a hurry to look at it that you never have time to do the dishes." "Those who hasten to live are in a hurry to miss." she sometimes used to whisper to Noah, though he didn't know what she meant before she was buried. Grandpa clasps his hands to stop them from shaking.

"When a brain fades it takes a long time for the body to realize. The human body has a tremendous work ethic; it's a mathematical masterpiece, it'll keep working until the very last light. Our brains are the most boundless equation, and once humanity solves it, it'll be more powerful than when we went to the moon. There's no greater mystery in the universe than a human. Do you remember what I told you about failing?"

"The only time you've failed is if you don't try once more."

"Exactly, Noahnoah, exactly. A great thought can never be kept on Earth."

Noah closes his eyes, stops the tears in their tracks, and forces them to cower beneath his eyelids. Snow starts to fall in the square, the same way very small children cry, like it had barely started at first but soon like it would never end. Heavy, white flakes cover all of Grandpa's ideas.

"Tell me about school, Noahnoah." the old man says.

He always wants to know everything about school, but not like other adults, who only want to know if Noah is behaving. Grandpa wants to know if the school is behaving. It hardly ever is.

"Our teacher made us write a story about what we want to be when we're big." Noah tells him.

"What did you write?"

"I wrote that I wanted to concentrate on being little first."

"That's a very good answer."

"Isn't it? I would rather be old than a grown-up. All grown-ups are angry, it's just children and old people who laugh."

"Did you write that?"

"Yes."

"What did your teacher say?"

"She said I hadn't understood the task."

"And what did you say?"

"I said she hadn't understood my answer."

"I love you." Grandpa manages to say with closed eyes.

"You're bleeding again." Noah says with his hand on Grandpa's forearm.

Grandpa wipes his forehead with a faded handkerchief. He's searching for something in his pockets. Then he looks at the boy's shoes, the way they swing a few inches above the tarmac with unruly shadows beneath them.

"When your feet touch the ground, I'll be in space, my dear Noahnoah."

The boy concentrates on breathing in time with Grandpa. That's another of their games.

"Are we here to learn how to say good-bye, Grandpa?" he eventually asks.

The old man scratches his chin, thinks for a long time.

"Yes, Noahnoah. I'm afraid we are."

"I think good-byes are hard." the boy admits.

Grandpa nods and strokes his cheek softly, though his fingertips are as rough as dry suede.

"You get that from your Grandma."

Noah remembers. When his dad picked him up from Grandma and Grandpa's in the evenings he wasn't even allowed to say those words to her. "Don't say it, Noah, don't you dare say it to me! I get old when you leave me. Every wrinkle on my face is a good-bye from you." she used to complain. And so he sang to her instead, and that made her laugh. She taught him to read and bake saffron buns and pour coffee without the pot dribbling, and when her hands started to shake the boy taught himself to pour half cups so she wouldn't spill any, because she was always ashamed when she did and he never let her feel ashamed in front of him. "The amount I love you, Noah," she would tell him with her lips to his ear after she read fairy tales about elves and he was just about to fall asleep, "the sky will never be that big." She wasn't perfect, but she was his. The boy sang to her the night before she died. Her body stopped working before her brain did. For Grandpa it's the opposite.

"I'm bad at good-byes." says the boy.

Grandpa's lips reveal all his teeth when he smiles.

"We'll have plenty of chances to practice. You'll be good at it. Almost all grown adults walk around full of regret over a good-bye they wish they'd been able to go back and say better. Our good-bye doesn't have to be like that, you'll be able to keep redoing it until it's perfect. And once it's perfect, that's when your feet will touch the ground and I'll be in space, and there won't be anything to be afraid of."

Noah holds the old man's hand, the man who taught him to fish and to never be afraid of big thoughts and to look at the night's sky and understand that it's made of numbers. Mathematics has blessed the boy in that sense, because he's no longer afraid of the thing almost everyone else is terrified of: infinity. Noah loves space because it never ends. It never dies. It's the one thing in his life which won't ever leave him.

He swings his legs, studies the glittering metals between the flowers.

"There are numbers on all the keys, Grandpa."

Grandpa leans forward over the edge and calmly looks at them.

"Yes, indeed, there are."

"Why?"

"I can't remember."

He suddenly sounds so afraid. His body is heavy, his voice is weak, and his skin is a sail about to be abandoned by the wind.

"Why are you holding my hand so tight, Grandpa?" the boy whispers again.

"Because all of this is disappearing, Noahnoah. And I want to keep hold of you longest of all."

The boy nods. Holds his grandpa's hand tighter in return.

He holds the girl's hand tighter and tighter and tighter, until she tenderly loosens one finger after another and kisses him on the neck.

"You're squeezing me like I was a rope."

"I don't want to lose you again. I couldn't go on."

She walks lightheartedly along the road next to him.

"I'm here. I've always been here. Tell me more about Noah, tell me everything."

His face softens bit by bit, until he's grinning and replies: "He's so tall now, his feet are going to reach all the way to the ground soon."

"You'll have to put more stones under the anchor then." she says with a laugh.

His lungs force him to stop and lean against a tree. Their names are carved into the bark, but he doesn't remember why.

"My memories are running away from me, my love, like when you try to separate oil and water. I'm constantly reading a book with a missing page, and it's always the most important one."

"I know, I know you're afraid." she answers and brushes her lips against his cheek.

"Where is this road taking us?"

"Home." she replies.

"Where are we?"

"We're back where we met. The dance hall where you stepped on my toes is over there, the café where I accidentally trapped your hand in the door. Your little finger is still crooked, you used to say that I probably only married you because I felt bad about that."

"I didn't care why you said yes. Just that you stayed."

"There's the church where you became mine. There's the house that became ours."

He closes his eyes, lets his nose lead the way.

"Your hyacinths. They've never smelled so strong."

For more than half a century they belonged to one another. She detested the same characteristics in him that last day as she had the first time she saw him under that tree, and still adored all the others.

"When you looked straight at me when I was seventy I fell just as hard as I did when I was sixteen." She smiles.

His fingertips touch the skin above her collarbone.

"You never became ordinary to me, my love. You were electric shocks and fire."

Her teeth tickle his earlobe when she replies: "No one could ask for more."

No one had ever fought with him like she had. Their very first fight had been about the universe; he explained how it had been created and she refused to accept it. He raised his voice, she got angry, he couldn't understand why, and she shouted, "I'm angry because you think everything happened by chance but there are billions of people on this planet and I found you so if you're saying I could just as well have found someone else then I can't bear your bloody mathematics!" Her fists had been clenched. He stood there looking at her for several minutes. Then he said that he loved her. It was the first time. They never stopped arguing and they never slept apart. he spent an entire working life calculating probabilities and she was the most improbable person he ever met. She turned him upside-down.

When they moved into their first house he spent the dark months growing a garden so beautiful that it knocked the air out of her when the light finally came. He did it with a determination only science can mobilize in a grown man, because he wanted to show that mathematics could be beautiful. He measured the angles of the sun, drew diagrams of where the trees cast their shade, kept statistics for the day-to-day temperatures, and optimized the choice of plants. "I wanted you to know." he said as she stood barefoot in the grass that June and cried. "Know what?" she asked. "That equations are magic, and that all formulas are spells." he said.

Now they are old and on a road. Her words against the fabric of his shirt: "And then you went about growing coriander in secret every year, just to mess with me."

He throws out his arms in a gesture of innocence.

"I don't know what you're talking about. I forget things, you know, I'm an old man. Are you saying you don't like coriander?"

"You've always known I hate it!"

"It must've been Noah. There's no trusting that boy." He laughs.

She stands on her tiptoes with both hands clutching his shirt and fixes her eyes on him.

"You were never easy, darling difficult sulky you, never diplomatic. You might even have been easy to dislike at times. But no one, absolutely no one, would dare tell me you were hard to love."

Next to the garden, which smelled of hyacinths and sometimes coriander, there was an old field. And there, right on the other side of the hedge, was a broken old fishing boat dragged up onto land by a neighbor many years earlier. Grandpa always said that he couldn't get any peace and quiet when he worked in the house, and Grandma always replied that she couldn't get any peace and quiet in the house when Grandpa was working there, so one morning Grandma went out into the garden and around the hedge and started to decorate the boat's cabin as an office. Grandpa sat there for years after that, surrounded by numbers and calculations and equations; it was the only place on Earth where everything was logical to him. Mathematicians need a place like that. Maybe everyone else does too.

There was a huge anchor leaning against one side of the boat. When Ted was very small, the boy would occasionally ask his dad how long it would be before he was taller than it. The dad has tried to remember when it happened. He's tried so hard that the square in his head quaked. He learned his lesson; he was a different man when Noah was born, became someone else as Grandpa than he had been as a father. That's not unique to mathematicians. When Noah asked the same question Ted once had, Grandpa replied: "You'll have to hope it never happens, because only people who are shorter than the anchor get to play in my office whenever they want." And when Noah's head began to approach the top of the anchor, Grandpa placed stones beneath it so he would never lose the privilege of being disturbed.

"Noah has gotten so smart, my love."

"He always has been, it just took you awhile to catch up," she snorts.

His voice catches in his throat.

"My brain is shrinking now, the square gets smaller every night."

She strokes his temples.

"Do you remember what you said, when we first fell in love, that sleeping was a torment?"

"Yes. Because we couldn't share our sleep. Every morning when I blinked awake, the seconds before I knew where I was were unbearable. Until I knew where you were."

She kisses him.

"I know that the way home is getting longer and longer every morning. But I loved you because your brain, your world, was always bigger than everyone else's. There's still a lot of it left."

"I miss you unbearably."

She smiles, her tears on his face.

"Darling stubborn you. I know you never believed in life after death. But you should know that I'm dearly, dearly, dearly hoping that you're wrong."

The road behind her is blurry, the horizon bearing rain. He holds her as hard as he can. Sighs deeply.

"Lord how you'll argue with me then. If we meet in Heaven."

A rake has been left propped against a wall. Lying next to it are three plant markers flecked with damp earth.

On the ground, there's a bag with a pair of glasses sticking out of one of its pockets. A microscope has been forgotten on a footstool and there's a white coat hanging from a hook, a pair of red shoes visible beneath. Grandpa proposed to her here, by the fountain, and Grandma's things are still everywhere.

The boy carefully touches the lump on Grandpa's forehead.

"Does it hurt?" he asks.

"No, not really." Grandpa replies.

"I mean on the inside. Does it hurt on the inside?"

"It hurts less and less. That's one good thing about forgetting things. You forget the things that hurt too."

"What does it feel like?"

"Like constantly searching for something in your pockets. First you lose the small things, then it's the big ones. It starts with keys and ends with people."

"Are you scared?"

"A bit. Are you?"

"A bit." the boy admits.

Grandpa grins.

"That'll keep the bears away."

Noah's cheek is resting against the old man's collarbone.

"When you've forgotten a person, do you forget you've forgotten?"

"No, sometimes I remember that I've forgotten. That's the worst kind of forgetting. Like being locked out in a storm. Then I try to force myself to remember harder, so hard that the whole square here shakes."

"Is that why you get so tired?"

"Yes, sometimes it feels like having fallen asleep on a sofa while it's still light and then suddenly being woken up once it's dark; it takes me a few seconds to remember where I am. I'm in space for a few moments, have to blink and rub my eyes and let my brain take a couple of extra steps to remember who I am and where I am. To get home. That's the road that's getting longer and longer every morning, the way home from space. I'm sailing on a big calm lake, Noahnoah."

"Horrible." says the boy.

"Yes. Very, very, very horrible. For some reason places and directions seem to be the first thing to disappear. First you forget where you're going, then where you've been, and eventually where you are…or…maybe it was the other way around…I…my doctor said something. I went to my doctor and he said something about, or did I say something. I said: 'Doctor, I…' "

He raps his temples, harder and harder. The square moves.

"It doesn't matter." the boy whispers.

"Sorry, Noahnoah."

The boy strokes his arm, shrugs.

"Don't worry. I'm going to give you a balloon, Grandpa. So you can have it in space."

"A balloon won't stop me from disappearing, Noahnoah." Grandpa sighs.

"I know. But you'll get it on your birthday. As a present."

"That sounds unnecessary." Grandpa smiles.

The boy nods.

"If you keep hold of it you'll know that right before you went into space someone gave you a balloon. And it's the most unnecessary present anyone can get because there's absolutely no need for a balloon in space. And that'll make you laugh."

Grandpa closes his eyes. Breathes in the boy's hair.

"That's the best present I've never been given."

The lake glitters, their feet move from side to side, trouser legs fluttering in the wind. It smells like water and sunshine on the bench. Not everyone knows that water and sunshine have scents, but they do, you just have to get far enough away from all other smells to realize it. You have to be sitting still in a boat, relaxing so much that you have time to lie on your back and think. Lakes and thoughts have that in common, they take time. Grandpa leans toward Noah and breathes out like people do at the start of a long sleep. one of them is getting bigger and one of them is getting smaller, the years allow them to meet in the middle. The boy points to a road on the other side of the square, blocked off by a barrier and a big warning sign.

"What's happened there, Grandpa?"

Grandpa blinks several times with his head against the boy's collarbone.

"Oh...that road...I think it's...it's closed. It washed away in the rain when your Grandma died. It's too dangerous to think about now, Noahnoah."

"Where did it go?"

"It was a shortcut. It didn't take long at all to get home in the mornings when I took that road, I just woke up and there I was." Grandpa mumbles and raps his forehead.

The boy wants to ask more, but Grandpa manages to stop him.

"Tell me more about school, Noahnoah."

Noah shrugs.

"We don't count enough and we write too much."

"That's always the way. They never learn, the schools."

"And I don't like the music lessons. Dad's trying to teach me to play guitar, but I can't."

"Don't worry. People like us have a different kind of music, Noahnoah."

"And we have to write essays all the time! The teacher wanted us to write what we thought the meaning of life was once."

"What did you write?"

"Company."

Grandpa closes his eyes.

"That's the best answer I've heard."

"My teacher said I had to write a longer answer."

"So what did you do?"

"I wrote: Company, and ice cream."

Grandpa spends a moment or two thinking that over. Then he asks: "What kind of ice cream?"

Noah smiles. It's nice to be understood.

He and the girl are on a road and they're young again. He remembers each of the very first times he saw her, he hides those pictures as far from the rain as he can. They were sixteen and even the snow was happy that morning, falling soap-bubble light and landing on cold cheeks as though the flakes were gently trying to wake someone they loved. She stood in front of him with January in her hair and he was lost. She was the first person in his life that he couldn't work out, though he spent every minute of it after that day trying.

"I always knew who I was with you. You were my shortcut." Grandpa confides.

"Even though I never had any sense of direction." She laughs.

"Death isn't fair."

"No, death is a slow drum. It counts every beat. We can't haggle with it for more time."

"Beautifully said, my love."

"I stole it."

Their laughter echoes in each other's chests, and then he says: "I miss all our most ordinary things. Breakfast on the veranda. Weeds in the flower beds."

She takes a breath, then answers: "I miss the dawn. The way it stamped its feet at the end of the water, increasingly frustrated and impatient, until there was no more holding back the sun. The way it sparkled right across the lake, reached the stones by the jetty and came onto land, its warm hands in our garden, pouring gentle light into our house, letting us kick off the covers and start the day. I miss you then, darling sleepy you. Miss you there."

"We lived an extraordinarily ordinary life."

"An ordinarily extraordinary life."

She laughs. Old eyes, new sunlight, and he still remembers how it felt to fall in love. The rain hasn't arrived yet.

They dance on the shortcut until darkness falls.

People are moving back and forth across the square. A blurry man steps on the dragon's foot, the dragon gives him a telling off. A boy is playing guitar beneath a tree, a sad tune, Grandpa hums along. A young woman walks barefoot across the square, stops to stroke the dragon. Her palms suddenly search her red coat, finding something in her pockets, something she seems to have spent a long time looking for. She looks up, straight at Noah, laughs happily and waves. As though he helped her to look, and she wants him to know he can stop now. That she's found it. That everything's okay. For a single moment he sees her face clearly. She has Grandma's eyes. Then the boy blinks, and she's gone.

"She looked like…" he whispers.

"I know." Grandpa nods, his hands move anxiously in his own pockets, then he lifts them up and lets his fingers move against his temples, like the outside of a box of raisins. Like he's trying to shake loose a piece of the past in there.

"I…she…that's your grandma. She was younger. You never got to meet her young, she has…she had the strongest feelings I ever experienced in a person, when she got angry she could empty a full bar of grown men, and when she was happy…there was no defending yourself against that, Noahnoah. She was a force of nature. Everything I am came from her, she was my Big Bang."

"How did you fall in love with her?" the boy asks.

Grandpa's hands land with one palm on his own knee and one on the boy's.

"She got lost in my heart, I think. Couldn't find her way out. Your grandma always had a terrible sense of direction. She could get lost on an escalator."

And then comes his laughter, crackling and popping like it's smoke from dry wood in his stomach. He puts an arm around the boy.

"Never in my life have I asked myself how I fell in love with her, Noahnoah. Only the other way around."

The boy looks at the keys on the ground, at the square and the fountain. He glances up toward space; if he stretches his fingers he can touch it. It's soft. When he and Grandpa go fishing they sometimes lie in the bottom of the boat with their eyes closed for hours without saying a word to one another. When Grandma was here she always stayed at home, and if anyone asked where her husband and grandson were she always said, "Space." It belongs to them.

It was a morning in December when she died. The whole house smelled of hyacinths and the boy cried the whole day. That night he lay next to Grandpa on his back in the snow in the garden and looked up at the stars. They sang for Grandma, both of them. Sang for space. Have done the same almost every night since. She belongs to them.

"Are you scared you're going to forget her?" the boy asks.

Grandpa nods.

"Very."

"Maybe you just need to forget her funeral." the boy suggests.

The boy himself could well imagine forgetting funerals. All funerals. But Grandpa shakes his head.

"If I forget the funeral I'll forget why I can't ever forget her."

"That sounds messy."

"Life sometimes is."

"Grandma believed in God, but you don't. Do you still get to go to Heaven if you die?"

"Only if I'm wrong."

The boy bites his lip and makes a promise: "I'll tell you about her when you forget, Grandpa. First thing every morning, first of all I'll tell you about her."

Grandpa squeezes his arm.

"Tell me that we danced, Noahnoah. Tell me that that's what it's like to fall in love, like you don't have room for yourself in your own feet."

"I promise."

"And tell me that she hated coriander. Tell me that I used to tell waiters in restaurants that she had a serious allergy, and when they asked whether someone could really be allergic to coriander I said: 'Believe me, she's seriously allergic, if you serve her coriander you could die!' She didn't find that funny at all, she said, but she laughed when she thought I wasn't looking."

"She used to say that coriander was a punishment rather than a herb." Noah laughs.

Grandpa nods, blinks at the treetops, and takes deep breaths from the leaves. Then he rests his forehead against the boy's and says: "Noahnoah, promise me something, one very last thing: once your goodbye is perfect, you have to leave me and not look back. Live your life. It's an awful thing to miss someone who's still here."

The boy spends a long time thinking about that. Then he says: "But one good thing with your brain being sick is that you're going to be really good at keeping secrets. That's a good thing if you're a grandpa."

Grandpa nods.

"That's true, that's true...what was that?"

Both of them grin.

"And I don't think you need to be scared of forgetting me." the boy says after a moment's consideration.

"No?"

The corners of the boy's mouth reach his earlobes.

"No. Because if you forget me then you'll just get the chance to get to know me again. And you'll like that, because I'm actually a pretty cool person to get to know."

Grandpa laughs and the square shakes. He knows no greater blessing.

They're sitting on the grass, him and her.

"Ted is so angry at me, love." Grandpa says.

"He's not angry at you, he's angry at the universe."

"He's angry because your enemy isn't something he can fight."

"It's a big universe to be angry with, a never-ending fury. I wish that he…"

"That he was more like you?"

"Less. That he was less like me. Less angry."

"He is. Just sadder. Do you remember when he was little and asked you why people went into space?"

"Yes. I told him it was because people are born adventurers, we have to explore and discover, it's our nature."

"But you could see that he was scared, so you also said: 'Ted, we're not going into space because we're afraid of aliens. We're going because we're scared we're alone. It's an awfully big universe to be alone in.' "

"Did I say that? That was smart of me."

"You probably stole it from someone."

"Probably."

"Ted might say the same thing to Noah now."

"Noah has never been afraid of space."

"That's because Noah is like me, he believes in God."

The old man lies down on the grass and smiles at the trees. She gets up and walks past the hedge, along the side of the boat, stroking it thoughtfully.

"Don't forget to put more stones under the anchor, Noah is growing so quickly." she reminds him.

The boat's cabin, the room in which he worked for so many years, looks so small in the twilight. Even though there was space for all his biggest thoughts. The lights are still there, the ones he strung up in a tangle on the outside of the boat so that Noah could always find his way if he woke up from a nightmare and needed to find his grandpa. A chaotic mess of green, yellow, and purple bulbs, as though Grandpa had been desperate for a poo when he put them up, so Noah would start laughing when he saw them. You can't be afraid of crossing dark gardens if you're laughing.

She lies down next to him, sighs with his skin close to hers.

"This is where we built our life. Everything. There's the road where you taught Ted to ride a bike."

His lips vanish between his teeth when he admits: "Ted taught himself. Like he taught himself to play guitar after I told him to stop messing about with it and do his homework instead."

"You were a busy man." she whispers, regret filling every word because she knows she bears the same guilt.

"And now Ted is a busy man." he says.

"But the universe gave you both Noah. He's the bridge between you. That's why we get the chance to spoil our grandchildren, because by doing that we're apologizing to our children."

"And how do we stop our children from hating us for that?"

"We can't. That's not our job."

He chases his breaths between throat and chest.

"Everyone always wondered how you put up with me, my love. Sometimes I wonder too."

Her giggles, how he misses them, the way they seemed to gain speed all the way from her feet.

"You were the first boy I met who knew how to dance. I thought it was probably best to seize the opportunity, who knows how often boys like that turn up?"

"I'm sorry about the coriander."

"No you're not, not at all."

"No, not at all, actually."

She carefully lets go of his hand in the darkness, but her voice still rests in his ear.

"Don't forget to put more stones under the anchor. And ask Ted about the guitar."

"It's too late now."

She laughs inside his brain then.

"Darling obstinate you. It's never too late to ask your son about something he loves."

Then the rain starts to fall, and the last thing he shouts to her is that he also hopes he's wrong. Dearly, dearly, dearly hopes. That she'll argue with him in Heaven.

A boy and his dad walk down a corridor; the dad holds the boy's hand softly.

"It's okay to be afraid, Noah, you don't need to be ashamed." he repeats.

"I know, Dad, don't worry." Noah says and yanks up his trousers when they slip down.

"They're a little bit too big, that was the smallest size they had. I'll have to adjust them for you when we get home." the dad promises.

"Is Grandpa in pain?" Noah wants to know.

"No, don't worry about that, he just cut his head when he fell over in the boat. It looks worse than it is, but he's not in pain, Noah."

"I mean on the inside. Does it hurt on the inside?"

The dad is breathing through his nose, and his eyes are closed, his steps slow down.

"It's hard to explain, Noah."

Noah nods and holds his hand more tightly.

"Don't be scared, Dad. It'll keep the bears away."

"What will?"

"Me wetting myself in the ambulance. That'll keep the bears away. There won't be any bears in that ambulance for years!"

Noah's dad's laugh is like a rumble. Noah loves it. Those big hands gently holding his small ones.

"We just need to be careful, does that make sense? With your grandpa. His brain…the thing is, Noah, sometimes it's going to be working slower than we're used to. Slower than Grandpa is used to."

"Yeah. The way home's getting longer and longer every morning now."

The father squats down and hugs him.

"My wonderful smart little boy. The amount I love you, Noah, the sky will never be that big."

"What can we do to help Grandpa?"

The dad's tears dry on the boy's sweatshirt.

"We can walk down the road with him. We can keep him company."

They take the lift down to the hospital parking lot, walk hand in hand toward the car. Fetch the green tent.

Ted and his dad are arguing again. Ted begs him to sit down, the dad furiously bellows: "I don't have time to teach you to ride your bike today, Ted! I told you! I have to work!"

"It's okay, Dad. I know."

"For God's sake, I just want my cigarettes! Tell me where you've hidden my cigarettes?" the dad roars.

"You stopped smoking years ago." says Ted.

"How the hell would you know?"

"I know because you stopped when I was born, Dad."

They stare at one another and breathe. Breathe and breathe and breathe. It's a never-ending rage, being angry at the universe.

"I... it..." Grandpa mumbles.

Ted's big hands hold his thin shoulders; Grandpa touches his beard.

"You've gotten so big, Tedted."

"Dad, listen to me, Noah is here now. He's going to sit with you. I just need to get a few things from the car."

Grandpa nods and rests his forehead against Ted's forehead.

"We need to go home soon, my boy, your mother's waiting for us. I'm sure she's worried."

Ted bites his lower lip.

"Okay, Dad. Soon. Really, really soon."

"How tall are you now, Tedted?"

"Six foot one, Dad."

"We'll have to put more stones under the anchor when we get home."

Ted is almost at the door when Grandpa asks if he has his guitar with him.

There's a hospital room at the end of a life where someone, right in the middle of the floor, has pitched a green tent. A person wakes up inside it, breathless and afraid, not knowing where he is. A young man sitting next to him whispers: "Don't be scared."

The person sits up in his sleeping bag, hugs his shaking knees, cries.

"Don't be scared." the young man repeats.

A balloon bounces against the roof of the tent; its string reaches the person's fingertips.

"I don't know who you are." he whispers.

The young man strokes his forearm.

"I'm Noah. You're my grandpa. You taught me to cycle on the road outside your house and you loved my grandma so much that there wasn't room for you in your own feet. She hated coriander but put up with you. You swore you would never stop smoking but you did when you became a father. You've been to space, because you're a born adventurer, and once you went to your doctor and said, 'Doctor, doctor! I've broken my arm in two places!' and then the doctor told you that you should really stop going there."

Grandpa smiles then, without moving his lips. Noah places the string from the balloon in his hand and shows him how he is holding the other end.

"We're inside the tent we used to sleep in by the lake, Grandpa, do you remember? If you tie this string around your wrist you can keep hold of the balloon when you fall asleep, and when you get scared you just need to yank it and I'll pull you back. Every time."

Grandpa nods slowly and strokes Noah's cheek in wonder.

"You look different, Noahnoah. How is school? Are the teachers better now?"

"Yes, Grandpa, the teachers are better. I'm one of them now. The teachers are great now."

"That's good, that's good, Noahnoah, a great brain can never be kept on Earth." Grandpa whispers and closes his eyes.

Space sings outside the hospital room; Ted plays guitar; Grandpa hums along. It's a big universe to be angry at but a long life to have company in. Noah strokes his daughter's hair; the girl turns toward him in the sleeping bag without waking up. She doesn't like mathematics, she prefers words and instruments like her grandpa. It won't be long before her feet touch the ground. They sleep in a row, the tent smells like hyacinths, and there's nothing to be afraid of.

图书在版编目（CIP）数据

在我离开之前 /（瑞典）弗雷德里克·巴克曼著；
余小山译 . — 2 版 . — 成都：四川文艺出版社，
2022.12
ISBN 978-7-5411-6480-4

Ⅰ.①在… Ⅱ.①弗… ②余… Ⅲ.①中篇小说－瑞典－现代 Ⅳ.① I532.45

中国版本图书馆 CIP 数据核字（2022）第 207095 号

And Every Morning the Way Home Gets Longer and Longer by Fredrik Backman
Copyright © 2017 by Fredrik Backman
Published by arrangement with Salomonsson Agency AB, through The Grayhawk Agency Ltd.
Simplified Chinese translation copyright © 2022 by Beijing Xiron Culture Group Co., Ltd.
All Rights Reserved.
著作权合同登记号 图进字：21-2020-127

ZAI WO LIKAI ZHIQIAN

在我离开之前

[瑞典] 弗雷德里克·巴克曼 著　余小山 译

出 品 人　张庆宁
责任编辑　王梓画
责任校对　段　敏

出版发行	四川文艺出版社（成都市锦江区三色路 238 号）		
网　　址	www.scwys.com		
电　　话	028-86361781（编辑部）		
印　　刷	北京盛通印刷股份有限公司		
成品尺寸	130mm×190mm	开　本	32 开
印　　张	4.25	字　数	86 千
版　　次	2022 年 12 月第二版	印　次	2022 年 12 月第一次印刷
书　　号	ISBN 978-7-5411-6480-4		
定　　价	48.00 元		

版权所有·侵权必究。如有质量问题，请与本公司图书销售中心联系调换。电话：010-82069336。